For Hire: Operator
By
Kevin A. Patterson
&
Alana Phelan

Jacq

Thanks for letting me be a geek for a day!

A For Hire Enterprises Publication

Cover and Interior Art by Miguel Blanco / IG: MrMiguelBlanco

ISBN: 978-1-7328728-0-6

This book is sort of a perfect storm of combined influences. So many of the interests and communities and identities that I'm a part of found their way into these pages. I'm eternally thankful to all the people who joined us along the way.

Kev

For Mahasin and Stevi, for all the loving support and advice over the years.

Allie

For Hire: Operator

Chapter One

"...as much as we love and live for hip hop, we've decided to take Flow House *in a new direction. With the awareness of Genetic Variance Syndrome, the rise of superhero culture, and now the introduction of extralegal operations, we've decided to rebrand as* For Hire. *Going forward we'll focus on the (estimated fifteen percent of) variants who live their lives outside the margins..."*

The final issue of Flow House *magazine — February 1991*

I was sitting alone in my favorite booth of my favorite pub in the lovely city of Cargill, N.J., eyes on the door as usual. And, as usual, the only people around were the regular customers Luke's Lockup always brought in. I meant to get a drink and to check my phone for emails but it stayed in my pocket as something else had my attention: my love, Marcella McKenzie. Beautiful, wondrous Marcella, commonly known as the glamorous and powerful superhero Double M, with her dark purple hair and matching heavy-grade armor I liked to rib her about. She didn't need that much protection, but she sure loved it and looked damn good in it. Unfortunately, my current view of her was limited to the cover of this month's *For Hire* magazine. Someone must have forgotten it in the booth. Ironic, really. This magazine cover was about as close to an evening out as Marcie and I would ever get together. She'd never be seen with me in public.

I glanced up and spied someone new entering the pub. *Interesting*, I thought, sipping my drink and flipping to the cover story. *For Hire* always treated my girl well, gushing over her latest triumph over some gang led by some variant while asking softball questions. As always, she dodged any details about her specific set of powers or their origins. She also dodged questions about her personal life. Shaking my head, I flipped to the last page, to the power rankings. There she was again, the number one superhero for the twenty-seventh month straight. It wasn't even a competition anymore, even though they'd all deny that the power rankings are anything but neutral information. Everybody is just out to serve justice. Sure. Right.

There were three paths to the type of superhumanity that might get you ranked. Genetic Variance Syndrome, or GVS, is an unexplained phenomenon that gives a small percentage of humans a randomized set of enhanced attributes. Marcella runs into criminal variants all the time. She described them like video game end-bosses. She beats her way through a gang before encountering the variant at the top. For the most part, their abilities are never a match for hers.

Marcella and I invented the second path to superhumanity, though nobody knows that but us. Well, almost nobody. Her fans assume her powers are a function of the armor she wears. If I had a more public persona, my fans would assume the same. Truth is, as teenagers, Marcella and I created something called Supercell: programmable nanotechnology that can accurately mimic human biological functions on a cellular level. As a result, our strength, speed, intelligence, and regenerative abilities are all off-the-charts powerful. Me and Marce are the only ones on the technology path.

The third path is magic which, up until recently, I didn't believe in. I set the magazine aside with one last glance at the cover before setting my sights on the source of the pub's sudden buzz.

The newcomer was loud, handsome, and covered in tattoos. Short and slight but with a huge presence, they had an easy smile and boisterous charm that I could spot even from a distance. Everyone at the bar recognized them the second they walked into the pub. I did, too, but not for the same reasons. The chances that they were here by coincidence were slim.

I ran a quick stock of my protection. Under my clothes, I wore my favorite set of light armor. It hugged my curves like spandex. Nothing bulky like that unwieldy crap Marce wore. It was breathable and flexible and held just enough defensive tech to ward off most blows that might hinder me as I fought or escaped. On my left hip was a silenced pistol. On my right thigh, a long knife. I could also conjure a hard-light shield from either hand. I took another sip of my drink. No use letting it go to waste.

After a round of selfies with the other patrons, the pub's newcomer looked directly at me. The chances that they were here by coincidence dropped to none. From a pocket, I slid out my cell phone, toggled over to the Supercell app, and double checked the settings on my nanites. Ready for action, if it came to that. The newcomer said something to the bartender and motioned in my direction.

The last time I'd seen them they were wearing a mask, but I had no doubt it was the same person. Two or three months ago they were magicking a sort of portal into existence while standing over a frightened man named Stanton—a man I'd been hired to kill. It was the first time I'd ever seen what could've only been magic, but I'm a professional. No time for gawking. I did what I was there to do before they could do what they were there to do. Long range, big gun, away without a trace. Or so I thought. Maybe I shouldn't be surprised that they found me. Right next to the superhero rankings, *For Hire* keeps a power ranking for operators, and they were number three in the country. Under the alias JC, though, I'm number one.

In the magazine, wearing the mask, they're simply called Voss13. To the rest of the general public and definitely to the slobbering fans at the bar, they're world-famous as the Amazing Magisteria, Marcella's favorite performer. She'll be pleased to know she was right about the magic being real.

Voss, as I'd come to think of them, picked up two frothy mugs from the bar and walked over to my booth. They set one mug in front of me, sat down, and gestured to the magazine I'd set aside. "Y'know Double M is my biggest fan?" They had a thick Australian accent. If overconfidence was an accent, they had that too. There was a fearless,

7

almost careless, grace to their movements, as if they'd never found a situation they couldn't charm their way out of. Even their look was crafted to draw people in: thrift store aesthetics created with top-tier designer labels. The illusion of relatability. Façade or no, it was pretty hot, and there was no way they didn't know it. It was obvious they felt in complete control of the situation. But so did I.

"Really?" I said, ignoring the new mug and sipping the drink I already had on hand. If they felt any way about the slight, they hid it well.

"Absolutely!" They took a huge belt of the mug they were holding, then set it down and brushed back their short, dark hair. "She's been following my career from the very beginning. She comes to see my show whenever I'm here in town. I even took her backstage a couple of times and showed her the real magic, if you know what I'm talking about!" They winked. I'd never seen someone so pleased with themself. But I guess banging a famous superhero like Double M is a pretty huge accomplishment even when you're already a colossal superstar. Of course, other than the fact that Voss and Magisteria are the same person, none of this was new information to me. Marcella and Magisteria had been rolling around with each other for at least a couple of years now, as many times as availability could afford their full-time mega-celebrity schedules.

"The real magic, huh? Like what you were doing with Stanton?"

"Aha! I knew it was you, JC, and I knew you would know it was me. Cheers!" They raised their glass in a toast and I returned it. No need to be overtly rude. I still didn't know the nature of this visit. "I wasn't exactly sure which one of you bastards fouled up my contract. Though I guessed." Suddenly, the gleam was gone from their dark eyes. The intensity almost made me miss a breath. "I wanted to talk to you about what you saw in your scope."

"I know tech, and what I saw wasn't tech. And then the great Magisteria themself comes walking into my bar. What other conclusion am I supposed to be drawing here?"

Voss nodded thoughtfully, looking me over, maybe coming to a decision. I tensed. "You know, most people don't believe in magic," they said slowly. "I only show mine to the rubes who think it's fake"—they hiked a thumb at the people by the bar—"or the poor sods who won't be around long enough to tell anyone that it's real. Which leaves you and I in a bit of a predicament."

"No worries, Voss. Your secret is safe with me. Call it professional courtesy." I smiled. "The only person I'm telling is my girlfriend. She's a huge fan of yours. We've been arguing for years about whether your tricks were real or not. To tell the truth, I'm kind of annoyed that you settled the debate in her favor. I won't give up any of your details, though. I'll just let her know that she won." Voss's grin returned at that, clearly proud to have gotten at least that one up on me. I can see why Marcella liked them. Even besides the looks, there was a magnetism to them. "What were you doing to Stanton anyway? If you don't mind my asking."

"You lost me a lot of money, JC." They took another big swig, casual again. But this time I wasn't buying it. "And a spot in the rankings. I was number two and now I'm playing catch up. But, as you say, professional courtesy." They paused and leaned in. A bit dramatically, I thought. Ever the performer. I could smell the beer, and something sweet underneath, on their breath. I leaned in closer without thinking. "I was making a portal to disappear our man to a cave at the bottom of the ocean." They saw my raised eyebrow and sat back, gesturing with a casual hand wave. "I went there on a scuba diving trip a few years ago and I've been leaving my empties there ever since."

"Kind of an elaborate way to kill someone isn't it? I prefer my method."

Voss took another quick look around the room. People were more interested in getting their Magisteria selfies online than in Magisteria themself. Still, they dropped their voice. "Here's the thing, JC: Clients don't hire me to kill people. They hire me to erase them. Gone with no trace and no witnesses. The investigation over Stanton's disappearance was supposed to delay the bit of legislation he was working on. His blatant assassination—your blatant assassination — made him a martyr, didn't it? The bill became unstoppable then. Even the opposition rushed it through. All in honor of a man that they couldn't stand even the day before. Funny how that works."

"So, how come you couldn't vanish his body or something?"

They spluttered laughing into their drink at that. "Erasing a person isn't hard. Erasing several scattered bits of a person takes time that I just didn't have. That's what your big gun left me. Along with a boom loud enough to wake the dead...or at least a compound full of armed guards. I barely had time to recharge and portal myself out of there before I was seen."

"Sorry about that. I didn't know all the details behind the job."

"You don't follow the story?" Voss said with wide eyes.

"Not really, no." I used to love knowing the details when I started as an operator. I was helping people and I always wanted to know how. But then there were the people that I wasn't helping, the targets. Even if stopping a bad person meant saving hundreds of innocent victims, I couldn't get over knowing about the loss that target's family suffered. The friends who lost a valued loved one. The charitable dealings that might disappear. So I acquired a list of clients that I knew would contract me for my definition of the greater good and then I stopped asking questions. I wasn't going to tell Voss13 all of that though.

"Well, I like having a bit of narrative to make the work interesting." They downed the rest of their drink, traced a finger around the rim of the mug, and smiled slyly. "You know, I figured we could see eye to eye professionally, but I wasn't sure. So I came here after revving myself up for a fight. Looks like that's not going to happen now. I've still got all this pent up energy. Any suggestions on how to work that out?"

This time it was me brushing their hair back from their face.

We closed out our tabs and were back at my apartment in only a few short minutes. Our kind of work, both as heroes and operators, tends to run us all tight. Most of us find a variety of ways to unwind after hours—batting cages, menial labor, underground fighting rings. For me and M, it's tinkering with our tech or fucking. The former we only do with each other. The latter, however...

Voss was as amazing as they publicly bill themself. From a pocket, they pulled out a wand and used it to instantly undo all the fasteners that held my armor in place. Even after learning that their powers were real, I still assumed the wand was a prop. Real magic, indeed. They had me floating up off the bed both literally and figuratively.

Safety and privacy concerns meant I almost never had sex with other operators, but if Marcella felt Magisteria could be trusted, I could take the risk. And it was certainly worth the reward.

I got under the covers to return the attention when the bedroom door opened. Voss and I both jumped at the sound.

Marcella wasn't paying attention as she walked in. It wasn't the first time one of us walked in while the other was fooling around. "Sorry, didn't know you had a guest...Magisteria?"

"Double M? The fuck is going on here?" Voss went from arching into my face to pushing me off with their feet. Despite the long-term relationship, they'd never spent time in our apartment before.

Throwing the blanket off my head, I turned to Voss and tried to play nonchalant, "I told you my girlfriend was a fan, didn't I?" In hindsight, it's a little flattering that they were so focused on me that they missed all the evidence that Marcella lived here. The trophies. The medals. The key to the city next to the photo of her shaking hands with the mayor.

I looked to Marcie. We trusted each other's judgment with the people we bring home. But this was still a bit of a strange case. "Magisteria happened into my favorite pub. I struck up a conversation about how much of a fan you are. One thing led to another and here we are. It's not a problem, is it?" I grinned.

She grinned back. "I don't know... is it a problem if I join?" Voss's eyes lit up. So, I settled back in between their legs and heard the muffled sounds of hulking armor hitting the floor as my girlfriend got herself undressed.

An hour later, Marcella headed off to shower and Voss started getting dressed. I didn't bother to do either. I had nowhere pressing to be. Operators set their own hours. Marce, though, was heading out on patrol tonight. She had only just stopped back home after her mentoring session to respond to some emails and grab a snack before clocking back in. Life of a government employee. Voss was still a superstar with a superstar's schedule and had to be up early the next morning. As the shower started, they turned that dazzling smile on me. "So... you and Double M, huh? I guess I've heard a lot about you then. She does tend to go on and on about her 'girlfriend this' and her 'girlfriend that.' I reckon I'm the first person to ever knowingly sleep with both power ranking leaders at the same time. I'm a goddamn legend! Why doesn't anyone know about you two?"

"She's a superhero, Voss. I'm an operator. You know how it is." I didn't need to tell them that my existence could hurt Marcie's squeaky-clean image or that her presence would shine a bright light on my mostly secret reputation. I watched Voss make those connections themself as they looked from me to the bathroom door and back to me again. And they were Marcella's person, not mine; I wasn't going to tell them that the only people who knew how close we are were our parents, our off the grid former friends, and the handful of people we've brought home to fuck together—always chosen by Marcella, none of whom left knowing how I get paid. I'd trusted her this long with our identities. I wasn't going to stop doing that just because I'd met one of her long-time fuck buddies.

"Fair enough. It's a situation that can get dicey, I guess. Thanks for covering for me, by the way. I wear a mask as Voss for a reason, y'know. Can't have the fans knowing what I do offstage." They put on a fancy printed binder and a very expensive looking pair of panties under a faded vintage band t-shirt, a heavy leather jacket, and rugged blue jeans. They nodded towards the bathroom door while putting on a worn pair of cowboy boots. "Especially my biggest fan. Me and her got the same operator/superhero dynamic, don't we? Only she doesn't know."

"Now you know something of mine and I know something of yours. Like I said, professional courtesy." More like mutually assured destruction, but Voss leaned in to give me a last kiss.

"Tell her I said goodbye, yeah? I put on a bit of a show about it back at the pub, but I like her. We're both too busy for us to have what

14

you have. But in another life, me and her might've been something more. With no real way to find out, I guess I'll just catch her at the next performance. Maybe I'll catch you too, yeah?" They winked. I blushed.

"Maybe," I said, and let myself smile. Then they were gone.

Chapter Two

"...it took almost a year of planning and effort, but as the public demanded, we've finally created a ranking system for both heroes and operators. Doing so for heroes was easy. The hard part was convincing the government to integrate our new methodology into the client/contractor service application. But we were able to prove its value to the employees, the employers, and to the entire industry surrounding extralegal operations. For our readers, we've added a rubric which can be found with a full explanation of the power rankings' implementation on page 26..."

For Hire *magazine — January 1997*

When she got out of the shower, Marcella didn't seem at all surprised that Voss was gone. She got dressed quietly—quietly enough to speak volumes. No updates about her day. No excited chatter about her upcoming patrol or her new mentees. Not even any residual gushing about the sex we just had. Finally, with everything on but the armor, she spoke. "A heads up would've been nice, Sana." Her voice was so level, so neutral, I wouldn't have recognized it if I hadn't been looking right at her.

"Since when do we give each other express notification that we're fooling around with somebody new?"

She gave me The Look. "That's not what this is about."

"If you're so worried, we exchanged health information on the way back from the pub. Plus, you already know their information. Right? Nothing new to report." I gave her a forced grin. I hoped she'd find the light tone cute, or charming.

Unfortunately, I didn't have even half of Voss's charm.

She crossed her arms in front of her. I almost laughed. It was an almost superheroic stance.

I spoke before she could. Always be on the offensive, right? "You bring people home sometimes. And this is someone you know."

"Exactly. They're not a random person. That's part of why I don't just bring them home. I know better and you should've too."

"Know better? Know better than what? It's not like I've ever been the one to do the choosing. Is this about me meeting one of your people, or one of your people meeting me?"

"I'm not ashamed of you. I just don't want you to treat someone meaningful to me like one of your throwaway one-night co-stars. It's not about your being an operator."

"Isn't everything though? Me being an operator is why I'm not a part of the rest of your life."

Her face fell, then tightened. "Don't put that on me. Maybe I hide your career for the sake of mine, but you've been hiding yourself a whole lot longer."

"I'm not hiding. I'm just living my life."

She made a frustrated noise that was almost a laugh. "What life? All you do is work and hang out at that pub all day. I *wish* your co-stars were more than that. At least then I'd know for sure that you're still capable of human connection beyond our relationship." She reached out to take my hand. I knew that she was trying to balance out the criticism, but I'm not like her. I can't feel all the things all the time. I gave her hand a squeeze but then let go.

"So what if I'm a workaholic? So are you. We were workaholics as teenagers and it hasn't changed now. It's just more job, less tech. And yeah, I'm an introvert. And? We can't all be extroverts. I don't meet people at the pub or on the job who I'd like to take home to meet my mom, or my girlfriend. Whatever. Who has time for that anyway? When I have the time, that energy goes to you."

"There's a difference between you being a teenaged introvert and you being a complete recluse as an adult. We both know what changed. Maybe we should talk about it instead of hiding from it."

I got out of bed and started pacing. "There's nothing to talk about. It happened, what the fuck can I do about it? Nothing. Be happy with who and what I got. I'm happy, Marce, I'm happy with you."

"Then let's hear more about this energy that goes to me. Tell me more about that. What did you do last night? Or the night before that? How do you even know Magisteria?"

"I told you, they were at the pub. We got to talking. I shot my shot."

"And you know what? All it would've taken was one text: 'Hey, Magisteria's at the pub! I'm shooting my shot. See you at home.' One moment of consideration. That's it. Walking in and finding a mostly-secret partner with their legs wrapped around the head of another mostly-secret partner wasn't exactly written on my calendar, by either of you." She pressed her lips together like she had more to say but wasn't going to let herself. Which meant what she was thinking about me wasn't pretty. That was fine, because I couldn't handle much more of this.

"I fucked up, okay? I see that now, but it's not like I broke a rule. I got caught up in a moment. I feel like I'm being punished for making a quick call—a call I made because I figured you and Magisteria had trust."

"You need to be checked in with me, Sana. Simply put, in this relationship you have one job to do: be present in our relationship. When you screw that up, it makes me feel like I'm just as unimportant to you as the rest of the world is."

"You're the most important thing," I told her, my voice firm.

She stood back up and picked up the last of her armor. "Thanks for saying that. I don't want to be late for patrol, but I'll be home right after."

"Hey," I said, and she faced me. "It's not the head's up that you wanted, but you'll be pleased to know the magic is real."

She stared at me for a long moment. "I know it's real, Sana. I always have."

19

Without another word, she walked out and let the door close heavily behind her.

And so it went. Don't ask, don't tell. When we'd started our lives in the big city, we were both heroes. I wanted us to wear masks and she wanted us to be public. She could never deal with my need for privacy and I couldn't mesh with her desire for fame. Fame? That sounds selfish, which isn't Marcie at all. What she wanted was to be a symbol to inspire good work in others. That's exactly what she has been too. I could respect it. I just couldn't be it. I didn't want to be a celebrity, I didn't want the attention. For the most part, I didn't want to be around people at all. I wanted to build miracle-tech. The equipment we used. The gear we wore. The Supercell nanites that have been running through our veins for the last seven years. Design, create, and utilize. That's what I loved and extralegal operations allowed me to do that.

About two years into our fledgling careers, I got an anonymous email asking to pay for my services. I was intrigued. Marcie didn't like it. "Operators are vigilantes at best...little better than straight up criminals" she said, but she still encouraged me to see where it went. Maybe she just wanted to be supportive. Maybe she thought I'd do one job and get it out of my system. We did enough research to ensure that the job was a net positive for the people it would affect. It was simple. Go to a place, capture a person, deliver them to a place designated by the client, profit! So I created an extralegal operations business account and accepted my first contract. Once I completed that mission, more came in. Before long I started having my pick of cushy jobs. I stopped going out on patrol. By the time Marce really made a name for herself, I was out of the hero biz entirely. When the first unofficial biography of Double M was released, I was barely even mentioned. There was a throwaway line in there about her starting her career with a partner before going solo. That's it. They didn't even use my cheesy superhero alias.

Off the page, we would still be together each night and chat about the details of our work. I thought she had gotten a better understanding of how I could still help people in a quieter way as an operator. I thought she had started to accept my place in the big picture. She was just putting on her supportive face to have my back. I didn't figure that out until I made my first kill. It was self defense, a clear-cut case of him or me. I cried like a baby for hours. Marcella consoled me all night. When I picked up another client the following morning, we got into a huge fight. "You're doing it again? What if you have to kill again? What if you're contracted to kill? Is this what you want? How does this help? Who does this serve?" It was probably the first real fight we'd had since high school.

We exploded at each other until our neighbors called in a noise complaint. When the police arrived, Marcie left. She climbed back in bed with me a few hours later. "I'm still mad at you, Sana. But when I'm mad, you usually make me feel better...so here we are." After that, we just stopped talking about my work. When I made my next kill, one I didn't have to make, I kept my peace. Good. No words said means no excuses made. Marce still regaled me with stories of her big wins and I celebrated her tremendous success. But I told her nothing and she quietly prayed for my safety...and I think for my soul. It's been that way ever since. My on-the-job highlight reel, including the five-star headshot that connected me to Voss, was just a silent film in my head. It had to be, for the sake of my relationship.

I wondered if my inbox held the next addition to that reel. I had to keep moving forward, and I had to distract myself from my girl. I cracked open my laptop and booted it up. Three emails were waiting for me. The first was a five-star rating and payment confirmation for my last contract: a long arduous takedown of a backwoods, anti-government militia group. People knew better than to stiff me on pay. I wasn't really doing this for money anyway. Seeing the rating in the subject line was all the info I needed.

Next up was a new contract from the same client. Same pay, same parameters, different militia group. Last time, I spent weeks hacking all their systems. I rearranged their finances and fabricated lines of communication that made the entire group suspect and then turn on one another. It was glorious watching it all play out at the end, but it felt like it took forever. I wasn't exactly eager to go back into that sort of slog. I declined the offer, sending it back into the contract pool. If I changed my mind later, I could always go back and see if it was still available.

Lastly, I had received a contract marked URGENT. The employer code indicated that it was from that first-ever client. My favorite client, the one I trusted the most—as much as you can trust in this business. Clear parameters. High pay. Reliable and succinct communication. A dream to work with. Work for this client was about as close as I ever got to dancing. I've never had to kill for them, but I would. When I hit the top of the rankings and decided to narrow down the list of people I'd continue accepting work from, this one was the easiest choice. I had already decided to take the contract before I even opened the email.

TIME SENSITIVE
356 Valley Avenue, Hewlett, North Carolina. Arrive at 4:55pm tomorrow evening and depart at 5:30pm. Observe everything. Report everything. Extensive notes. Engage with no one. Tell no one. Payment information follows.

This was a little vaguer than I was used to, but not alarmingly so. I accepted the contract and looked up flight information. There was a departure at noon from Cargill International. I could land in Raleigh, North Carolina at 1:30pm, rent a car, and be in Hewlett by 3pm. That gave me lots of time to scope out the surroundings and plan multiple exits before the observation period started. According to the search results, the address was a bowling alley. Across the street was a diner with pie that won an award at this year's county fair. It was like the job was planning itself.

This was what I loved about my life: I work how I want to work. I fuck who I want to fuck. I'm rich, extremely successful, and I live free

23

from people who might betray or abandon me. It's just me, the tech, the job, and Marcella. I smiled as I closed my laptop and called it a night.

We'd be fine, Marcie and me. We always had been. We always would.

Chapter Three

When asked about the historic nature of extralegal operations'
acceptance into American culture, historian Dr. Carly Steif responded,
"It's not unprecedented by any means. It's only historic in that it's been
done endlessly throughout history. Alcohol was legal until it wasn't.
Then it was illegal until it wasn't. We talk about the sanctity of life on
one hand. Yet, on the other, in guns we glorify a device that only has the
singular purpose of killing people. If I sell you heroin, I'm a drug dealer. If
I sell you tar and nicotine, which is more than thirty times as deadly, I'm
a businesswoman. Anyone who was shocked at the acceptance of
extralegal operations hadn't been paying attention."

— For Hire *magazine* — *April 2005*

The next morning I got an early start. I always did on game day,
even when the contract didn't require it. I don't know when Marcella
finally came home but I woke up with her arms around me just like most
mornings. Even when she's mad at me, she tries her best to reconnect. I
wanted to kiss her before I left. I usually did. But if I woke her up, the
same argument from last night might spark back up. I needed to keep
my focus on the upcoming job. So I slid out from her arms, got dressed,
and skipped out as quietly as I could. I sent her a text message to let her
know I'd be out of town most of the day. I didn't expect her to respond

once she woke up. She always wanted to know I was safe, but she never wanted to appear to condone whatever I was doing.

Breakfast was eggs, ackee, saltfish, and fried dumplings from the nearby Jamaican restaurant. Mom would be proud. I took some time during my meal to review the job details, such as they were. Location and mission parameters—that's all I had to go on. There wasn't even any real information about the bowling alley other than its existence. The website had an exterior shot of the building, a stock photo of a white man bowling, and the usual details on driving directions and the cost of shoe rentals. I couldn't even find a league schedule or events calendar. My first thought: it's a front. Maybe that's why I was going there to investigate in the first place.

No problem. I was a professional. I'd finish this food and do what I was being paid to do.

I hailed a cab and made my way to the airport. There was always a certain glamour I felt when I was heading to work out of Cargill. This was technically my version of a morning commute, but this wasn't a packed bus on the way to a boring job that I hate. I wasn't taking the subway across town to sit in a cubicle for eight hours. I was heading toward a life of adventure. Sure, I was only heading to a sleepy Southern town I've never heard of just to observe. Who knows though? The job can be unpredictable. Parameters can change up on the fly once I got there. It'd happened before. I might need to shoot my way out of that bowling alley and speed off into the night to escape that sleepy

Southern town. I might be heading directly into a scene out of a movie. Stuff like that always made me feel like an action hero.

That feeling carried all the way through to the airport gate when I sat down and found myself deflating a bit. Too little information about the job meant too much time to think, so of course my thoughts drifted to Marcella. It was a shame that I couldn't really share how I felt with her. She wouldn't want to hear how small the people around me feel when I'm on the job. These flight attendants and baggage handlers and food prep workers weren't heading off to potentially create some dramatic shift in this country's landscape. I was. But if I said that to the only relevant person in my life, she'd remind me that these are exactly the folks she fights the hardest for and therefore they were the ones who mattered the most. And they love her for that. I'd seen at least five kids wearing Double M merchandise since I arrived here and there was a commercial for her energy drink playing on an overhead monitor. I felt both saddened and relieved that I couldn't really hear it from where I was sitting.

I stifle a bit of a laugh as the next commercial began to play. It was for The Amazing Magisteria's upcoming nationwide tour. Tickets were going on sale soon. They'd sell out almost immediately, I was sure. They nearly always did. The stifled laugh turned into a sigh as I returned to my previous thoughts. Magisteria would understand. In or out of their identity as Voss13, they knew what it meant to feel larger than life. Our time together was brief and mostly sexual, but our conversations pre- and post-threesome were the only times I've spoken out loud about being an operator in years. Those might have been the first times I'd discussed the topic freely with someone who would really understand: a colleague who'd get the logistics of a contract, conflicting ideologies and methodologies on completing a set task, the blowback that the job can have on your personal life. As far as fleeting encounters go, that one provided a lot more value than I would've expected. But my sudden warm fuzzies over Voss were interrupted by the announcement of the flight boarding.

I drifted in and out during the flight, my thoughts and dreams a jumble of me, Marcie, and Voss.

The flight landed on time, but the car rental took far longer than I expected. I don't know why rental places even took reservations if they couldn't bother to have your car ready when you arrive. It's hard to continue feeling like an action hero while waiting for one of those supposed little people to finish vacuuming out the car you're heading off to change the world in. I did use the delay to suit up though. My body armor may have looked like a catsuit, but it was still based on the same nanotechnology that was running through my veins. The hard light and levitation tech were both identifiable by standard metal detectors. There was no way I could get on a plane wearing gear like that, not without the security pre-approval that came with a superhero license. So I had to pack both the armor and weaponry in my checked luggage. It's also hard to continue feeling like an action hero while changing into armor in a public restroom stall at the airport.

By the time I was ready to go, my car was finally available. The drive ran into a few pockets of traffic. I didn't arrive in the small town of Hewlett until almost quarter to four. Just long enough to get a meal and a plate of that award-winning pie at the diner before I had to move across the street and start the clock.

I found a seat by the front window and took in the sights. There weren't many, but the bowling alley was jumping. There was a big event there tonight for sure. There were lots of red, white, and blue banners and dozens of people were streaming in. With about ten minutes to spare, I paid my bill and headed across the street. For the record, the pie deserved that award.

The air inside the bowling alley was thick and moist from the heat of the crush. There was barely room to move and it was too loud to overhear a conversation. I was lucky to slide into a seat as soon as someone got up. Good. I began taking notes on my tablet.

Just after five, it became clear what—or rather, who—the focus of the event was. The general buzz became a murmur as a tall black man completed a game in the first lane. I could only just see the top of his head from where I sat, but I could clearly see the score on the monitor overlooking the lane. He was good. Really good. After completing a 263 game, he turned to address the crowd. "I'd like to thank everyone for coming out tonight to raise funds for this movement. But the movement isn't just mine. It belongs to you. It belongs to all of us!"

As he spoke, he moved through the crowd, up out of the bowling area, heading to a point where I could see him. But I knew I didn't have to. I knew that voice. I knew it better than I knew my own. Almost as well as I knew Marcella's. I would know that face too.

I was frozen. Me, JC, top of the operator rankings, frozen in place. Eyes transfixed on his path, the path that would reveal him to me for the first time in seven years.

"Over the last few years, we've turned around Hewlett...and the county...and the entire area! We've revitalized the local economy. We thumbed our noses at the officials that couldn't help our job creation when we created our own industries, right here in town. From reopening the plant across town all the way to celebrating Florence's award-winning pies right across the street, Hewlett has become a hub of new growth! With your support, I'd like to take the culture we've created right here and use it to turn around the whole state! When North Carolina becomes the lead state in this great country, the stories will say that it started right here in Hewlett!"

The crowd went wild...and I'd never seen Mark Jeffers look more beautiful. Seven years and he'd gone from looking like a boy to a man. His hair was still closely cropped but his face had thinned out a bit, making him look more mature. It was clear that he had put on several pounds of muscle. His shirt and tie couldn't hide it. He was wearing the kind of physique specifically honed through years of intense physical labor. Seven fucking years of it. I'd given up on looking for him after the first two. I'd stopped holding out hope that I'd ever see him again. Now my high school ex-boyfriend and I were in the same place again and I felt like I was gonna be sick.

I focused on taking the rest of my notes to keep from leaving the pie I ate on the floor in front of me. I had no idea if the notes were coherent, but they were helping. Mark made his way in my general direction. He was shaking hands and meeting all his constituents.

The energy in the place was unbelievable. This was a political rally in a random bowling alley in Nowhere, U.S.A., but it felt like what I imagine a Magisteria show at Madison Square Garden would feel like. It wasn't the crowd either. It was him. It was Mark. That smile that lit up a room. The earnestness in his eyes. The confidence to make believers out of a whole room of people all at once.

When he got near to me, I got up as casually as I could and waded through the bodies and into the nearest restroom. Though it was gender neutral, I thought it unlikely that he'd follow me in here during this big moment. I needed a minute to compose myself. I took a deep breath, splashed some water on my face, and breathed out. Marginally better. Trying to regain focus, I glanced at my watch. 5:35. I had to get out of there, and not just because of the mission parameters. I needed to be gone. I cracked open the door and glanced out in the sea of people. Mark was on the far end of the alley taking pictures with babies. I wanted to laugh. But if I did, my already-unsettled stomach wouldn't be able to take the jolt.

I was able to slip out of a side entrance and make it over to my rental car without incident. The GPS was already set for the airport and my flight would be leaving in a little more than two hours. The drive felt more frantic than it really was. The car wasn't moving nearly as fast as my thoughts. I hadn't seen Mark since he and the rest of our friends ghosted on Marcella and me back when we were eighteen. When I knew him last, he was an artist with no interest in politics. A nerd/jock who got his head in the game only for the game. Otherwise, like Marcie and me, he was creating, always creating. He had even designed the user interface for the app I still used to control my nanites.

But now, especially now, that felt like a lifetime ago. Back when Supercell was a still team. Back when he and I loved each other. Back when I let myself feel anything for anyone that wasn't Marcella. Now Mark was running for a spot in the U.S. House of Representatives out of some podunk town in North Carolina?

None of this made any sense to me. I was trying to connect the dots. As I drove, I had the tablet read and reread back all the notes I took. I used voice commands to scour the web for as much information as I could find. Years had passed since the last time I used my resources to look for the people who had abandoned us. Had Marcella and I maintained our search, we'd have found Mark almost two years ago. Not only had he just appeared on the scene of local government back in Hewlett then, but he'd started to make waves as a factory worker who eventually became a union leader. Or so the character profiles all said on his search results. Like he'd said at the bowling alley, he led a people-focused turnaround to the area businesses. Everywhere he set his eyes saw a positive gain. With his natural charm and his Supercell enhancements, I wasn't at all surprised. After several polite declines, he eventually ran for office at the behest of his supporters. Everyone said he was on the rise. Clearly!

The more information I took in, the more I calmed down and let my operator brain take over. This wasn't about putting me in a room with my ex. How could it be? So something bigger was going on. I did the thing I'd told Voss I no longer did: I followed the story.

I stopped chasing Mark's information and had the tablet's voice assistant read me the details on Hewlett. Eventually, it all clicked into place. The town was a strategic goldmine. North Carolina is a political battleground state and, though apparently inconsequential, Hewlett was the cornerstone of a cluster of small towns that helped turn the county and ultimately the entire state towards majority support for the current unpopular president. If Mark could flip these towns, he could flip the whole state and possibly the whole next presidential election. Given his track record and the charisma I'd seen back at the bowling alley, it seemed more than likely that he'd do exactly that.

But someone hired me to scope him out. In fact, my favorite and most reliable client contracted me to scope him out. But were they looking to help Mark's cause or to hurt it...or him? My brain started racing again. Maybe I shouldn't turn in the report. Maybe I should tell Marcella. Both violated my mission protocols, but did I even care about that right now?

At the airport, I returned the rental car, put my gear back in my luggage, and checked my email. I had received a new message in my inbox from about half an hour before. It was the client.

What the fuck was I supposed to do here? My time as an operator had been stellar thus far. I've made a ton of money and built a reputation for efficiency and professionalism. I'd been number one on *For Hire*'s rankings for three straight months. Even cracking the top ten was a huge achievement and I'd been there for a year and a half. There were allowances that could be made for having a contract intercepted by another operator, as had happened with Voss. But failing a contract or cancelling it midstream would fuck my elite status completely. I'd be back to getting B- and C-List contract offers again.

This was Mark, though. Why was I considering damaging my standing for a guy that walked out on relationships with both me and Marcella? Just like the rest of our former friends, he still had our nanotechnology in his body. All this time, he'd been thriving off our inventions and probably our initial funding as well. Did I have enough of an intact heart to give a fuck about him? If I didn't, it's because he broke that heart into a million pieces when he left. They all did.

...This was Mark, though. What if he was in danger? I'd been contracted to observe targets that I was later contracted to hurt or kill. Never by this client, but what if that changed? Of course, I'd decline the contract, but someone wouldn't. The image of Mark drowning in some underwater cave flooded into my brain. Of Voss13 casually calling my oldest friend one of their 'empties' while in bed afterglowing with some fuckbuddy.

I couldn't do it. I couldn't just turn in the report and possibly set off a chain of events that would end Mark's life. I needed the story; I needed to know it all. But I couldn't think of a way to pull that off, not in a way that would satisfy both me and the client, that would allow me to stay number one. I needed time. Fortunately, I had a couple hours in a plane to plan, and a client I'd never let down before. I decided to take the risk and respond to the message right away, in case the client had a read receipt on the email.

Complications arose, I wrote. *Will send full report upon landing.*

The response came immediately.

Report in person. Travel information follows

What in hell...?

Chapter Four

"It's not a stretch to say that I'm a dreamer. My parents could've shut that down but instead they encouraged it. When I was drawing spaceships in high school, my friends tried to help me build them. When I became a superhero, legends like Frank Curry gave me advice. That's why I started up my training program. I want to help other dreamers."

—Double M in For Hire *magazine — July 2018*

It was only six words, but I read the response a dozen times. In five years, I'd never met any of my clients. It'd never even been suggested by either party. I stared at my phone until a new email arrived: confirmation of an upcoming flight, in only forty-five minutes but two gates away from the original. It was coded to my operator alias, Jace Clementine.

I'd only just left the rental place and hadn't gotten my boarding pass yet. I could just turn in the new info and board this flight to...Ohio? Of all the places my favorite client might have been working out of, Ohio wouldn't have been any of my guesses.

But was it some sort of trap? Nobody would know if I changed flights now, including the only person I'd even want to tell. If Marcella eventually came looking for me, she'd only find my previous flight info and a plane back to New Jersey that I was never on.

But even if it was a trap, I didn't want Double M involved. Not only because of the messiness that would entail—my girl's superheroics are not subtle—but because of Mark.

I had my personal equipment in my luggage. I'd land, gear up, learn the situation, and murder this son of a bitch if he wants to hurt my friend. Ex-friend. Whatever. Then I'd go home and tell Marcella. And then we'd go back to Hewlett, North Carolina, and punch Mark Jeffers in the fucking face.

Decision made.

Sana: *Working overtime. Back tomorrow probably. Love you.*
Marcella: *Love you too. Please be safe*
Sana: *I will*

I won't, I would have written if I thought I could be honest with her. This is the opposite of safe. But this is where we are right now. Let's see how it plays.

I spent the entire hour-plus flight angry. Not just with the situation or the client but with Mark as well. I don't make friends easily; that's no surprise to anyone who's met me. But I wasn't always this...guarded. People let me down. Mark was one of them. We'd been

37

partners, and not just romantically. He'd been one of the people involved in the creation of Marcella's and my nanotechnology. Her spark, our work. Mark and the others—all of us high schoolers but brilliant even before the enhancements, if I do say so myself—helped during the implementation phase and were rewarded with a lower grade version of the tech we perfected together. Their nanites weren't customizable or adjustable but brought them to the peak of human potential.

Then they disappeared, leaving holes in our hearts and samples missing from our lab.

The only sign they'd ever been there at all, other than the result of their work, was a cryptic note:

See you at Phase Two.

By the time the plane landed, I was in Fuck This Shit mode. Or Fuck Shit Up mode. Either would work. I made a beeline right to the baggage claim to wait for my gear. Just as it arrived and I took the bag off of the belt, a young man stepped up and greeted me. He was a cute guy of Asian descent with cool spiky hair. He looked to be maybe eighteen or nineteen. No way he was the driver. "Hello? Miss Clementine? I'm Ronnie. I'll be your driver today." I looked down at my phone. *Driver will meet you at baggage claim...* Fine. I could kill this guy too if I needed to.

"Nice to meet you, Ronnie," I said, which we both knew was a lie. "Give me a second to hit the restroom and I'll be ready to go."

"No problem. I can take your bag out to the car." He reached for my luggage then stopped at the look that I gave him.

"I don't like people touching my stuff, Ronnie. No offense."

"None taken. I'll just wait right here for you." His smile never wavered. Either I was even angrier than I thought, or he had a very punchable face.

"Thank you."

Ten minutes later, I was geared up and sitting in the backseat of a random SUV. It was Ronnie's personal car. "You could've sat up front with me," he said.

"I'm not really sure what the protocol is for this sort of thing. I don't get many airport pickups."

"Well, I don't do this a lot either. Airport pickups, I mean. I'm just doing a favor."

"A favor for whom, Ronnie? Who do you work for?"

"Ummm...is this a test? I assumed we worked for the same person. I was just asked to pick you up and bring you back to the rec center." Ronnie sent a text message at the next red light and got a quick response. "He says it doesn't matter, since you're about to meet the man himself. I work for Mr. Frost. He says I can answer some of your questions."

"Really? What kind of business does Mr. Frost do?"

"He hacks. We all hack. We uncover waste, fraud, and abuse. Corruption of all kinds."

"Any money in that?"

"Lots! Each of us pockets ten percent of any money we're able to recover from the corrupt bastards stealing it. The rest goes back to the budget where it belongs. Except after our interventions, the people in charge of those funds know we're watching. So, they know not to use those funds improperly going forward." He took a deep swallow before continuing. "So, does that make you a... contractor? Like an operator?"

Time to put the fear of God in this guy. "That's sharp, Ronnie. I didn't expect you to be smart."

"Why not?"

"Because you're collecting ten percent of recovered cash and you're still driving this piece of shit SUV. Low man on the ladder, huh? Is that why you're running errands instead of bringing down scumbags?"

"I assumed you'd be a bitch because of what you do, but wow! Not that it's any of your business, but most of my money goes back into Mr. Frost's rec center. We're really making a difference there and I want to make sure it thrives. I'm running errands because Mr. Frost trusts me to do the stuff he needs a personal touch with. And I don't bring down scumbags...that's your job."

I was starting to like this kid. He knows I could end him, but he chose to talk back anyway. His face seemed more likable and less punchable now. It wouldn't matter if push came to shove, but Frost was lucky to have such a loyal kid on his side.

We arrived at the rec center after maybe thirty minutes of driving. Good to know we were still close to the airport for when it was time to leave. Except for its large size, the rec center was exactly what every rec center was. When we walked in, I was immediately assaulted by the smell of physical activity: sweat, chlorine, cleaning products. Through a closing door, I caught a brief glimpse of a locker room area. In a window just past the information desk, I saw a large swimming pool. Down the main hallway, I saw a pair of young people chatting while wearing boxing gloves laced behind their heads. I couldn't see the courts, but I could distinctly hear at least two basketballs bouncing and sneakers squeaking on hardwood floors. This place was massive.

Ronnie was popular. He knew everyone's name. He shook hands and high-fived everyone we saw as he led me to a back room beyond the administration area. First, we passed through a laundry room, then a server room, then stopped in a room full of computer workstations. Several young men and women were hard at work. None looked up, but a couple greeted Ronnie. One called out, "How'd our boy sound, JC?" I recognized his British accent immediately. Still short, still chubby, still wearing the same fucking glasses.

"You fucking bastard!" I yelled at my old friend and betrayer Darryl Hicks-Brand.

Chapter Five

"Oh my god! Where do I start? I guess logically with Franklin Curry's demand to change the racial demographic of law enforcement in Cleveland. Or the Holliday Sisters' push for gender equal pay in Atlanta. Or the changes to how Boston deals with housing based on ACOG Ultra's work. Superheroes have been great for stopping crime and rescuing cats out of trees and all that. But their real impact has always been enacting positive social change and inspiring their communities."

Historian Dr. Carly Steif — For Hire *magazine* — *October 1998*

I wasn't sure whether to hug him or punch him. My body felt like it was locked in combat—a rush of adrenaline paralyzed me, but I could feel the other chemicals battling it out. What was I feeling? Anger. Love. Fear. My stomach was doing flips. "I can't believe you. It's been you all this time? After seven goddamn years...and that's all you have to say for yourself, D—"

"Easy now, love. Don't use the name. In here, I'm Frost. Mr. Frost." He looked to Ronnie. "I really appreciate this. I'm putting some bonus money in your account, this week. Spend it on yourself. That's an order." He gave him a hug and then looked back to me. "Let's go shoot some hoop."

"Are you kidding?"

He wasn't.

"What? Don't think you can ball with all that armor on?" He laughed, looked me up and down, and threw a few light punches at me. I was well into defending myself before I realized he was just play-boxing with open hands. "It's great to see you again. I've really missed you. Both of you. C'mon." Then he turned on his heel and headed towards a door I hadn't noticed before.

I was already keyed up pretty high before I arrived, but his nonchalance was dialing me up even further. Two long lost friends in the same day. One a rising star politician in a tiny Southern shithole and the other a hacker based out of some Midwestern rec center, while also being my most steady client. And now, after several years of abandonment and unanswered questions, I was being led to a basketball court?

As if we were still just a group of teenagers creating tech magic in a basement lab.

As if they didn't all just vanish five minutes after helping Marcella and I achieve our goals.

As if Darryl hadn't been leading me by the nose for my entire career as an operator.

Now I wanted to do the leading. I could hear soft thuds in the distance and remembered the chatting kids I saw earlier. I clapped Darryl on the shoulder, gripped hard, and directed him away from the courts.

"What are you doing?"

"It's just...I've missed you so much, Mr. Frost." I added a sarcastic bite to his alias. I wanted him to read my contempt and contemplate where it might lead. "I'm just so happy to see you again that I feel like dancing."

I physically steered him towards the sound of the thuds, kicked open a door and saw far more than I expected. In my head I had envisioned a single crappy boxing ring, which would've been enough for my needs. What I found was a large gym area dedicated to combat sports in general. A boxing ring was present, but it wasn't crappy. It was almost professional grade and in great condition. There were also shelves filled with well-maintained gloves of varying weights. Racks of kickboxing pads. Rows of freestanding heavy bags and speed bags. Even a pair of wooden training dummies, both the original Wing Chun type and the modified Jeet Kune Do version. In a far corner, I spotted my new destination: an eight-sided, fence-enclosed mixed martial arts ring.

I drew the attention of every pair of eyes in that place as I forced their big boss past all the training mats and over towards the octagon. A couple of members seemingly ran out to get help. There were already a pair of young people sparring in the ring when we got there. They couldn't have been older than fifteen.

"Get out of here, kids! The grown folks gotta have a chat," I said as I freed a hand to open the gate.

Darryl struggled a bit, but I tightened my grip and he settled down. Had I been almost anyone else, he'd have been able to break free of my hold and subdue me. But I wasn't almost anyone else. As strong

44

as his nanites made him, he was still within the range of human capability. I was well outside of that range. I tossed Darryl into the ring and made room for the scared youngsters to leave before I shut and latched the door behind us.

"Love! I'm taking your meaning here. You're upset," he said. "But I'm not sure I understand why. Can we just talk?"

"You're not sure you understand why? Okay. Defend yourself, Frost!"

There would be time for talking. But first we had to make time for this.

He forced a conciliatory smile. "Need I remind you, Ms. Clementine, that I'm a lover not a fighter?"

"I don't remember you being much of either back in the day, honestly. But if you're worried about messing up some current reputation you've built up, don't be. This isn't going to be a fight." His face dropped and that was my cue to punch him in the stomach.

He doubled over in pain and fell to all fours. "Nice one, love. Nice one. Get it all out of your system yet?" He coughed out and held up a pleading hand.

With my left hand, I grabbed his shirt by the collar and dragged him up to his feet. With my right, I slipped off his glasses and casually flicked them over my shoulder, where they landed on the springy canvas with barely a sound. "Not. Even. Remotely!" Each word punctuated with a hard slap to the face. I don't know why I was slapping instead of punching. Maybe I didn't want to cause him any lasting or

45

more serious damage. Maybe I just wanted him to take more hits before I was through.

"Seven. Goddamn. Years?"

Each impact could be heard in every corner of this gymnasium. The sound drowned out the other activity of the place. Or maybe everyone just went quiet when their beloved owner started getting his ass kicked.

All my hurt and frustration were pouring out as I threw Darryl face first into the fence. I'd been carrying them around since four of my only five friends abandoned me. And now I was hand delivering them right back to the source. It felt cathartic...but he was making this too easy. "FUCKING DEFEND YOURSELF!" My voice sounded raw. I heard the pain in it, and I took a quick look around to see who else may have caught it. Our audience stood open-mouthed. They were clueless, even about me. Good.

He rolled over onto his back then used the fencing to sit up. Wheezing heavily and bleeding from the mouth, he said in a low voice, "I can't, Sana. I would...but I can't. You're too fast and too strong. It's not even worth the attempt." Something in the way he used my first name gave me pause. Enough of a pause that I didn't notice that a third person was opening the gate and stepping into the octagon.

"LEAVE HIM ALONE!" It was Ronnie and he was holding a gun. Two hands. Feet shoulder length apart. Knees slightly bent. Barrel aimed directly at my chest. Center mass. Good form. The kid had had some training. Not that it mattered. At most, he'd get off a single round before I disarmed him and made him eat that gun. Besides my speed, I'd had my hard-light shielding turned on since the airport. The speed and kinetic energy of a bullet would activate it and deflect the shot. If he hit me, even at this range, I'd barely feel it.

"Don't shoot!" Darryl struggled to his feet to plant himself between me and his young assistant. "Put it away, Ronald. We've still got kids about. Plus, it's fine. We're just a couple of mates catching up. No big deal. Right?" he spat out a mouthful of blood and looked to me for confirmation. "Tell him we're friends, JC."

He had blood on his chin and tears in his eyes and here he was pleading with a loyal soldier to accept our friendship. So much consideration for this kid and members of this center. So much more consideration than Marcie and I got when they left. It should have been a turning point, seeing him vulnerable, knowing he could care after all. Instead, I felt a fresh wave of rage. Seeing his obvious affection for this young man, who was around the same age as we all were when he disappeared, and how he was willing to protect him no matter what—it felt like confirmation of how little he cared about Marcie and me back when. Still, I didn't attack again. If I decided to continue beating him, he'd accept it. To sate my rage, he'd quietly let me beat the life out of him. It would be a loss for me, of answers and my pride.

I turned from Darryl back to the kid. Was that the same hero worship I'd had seven years ago? And how would he feel if I took away someone he cared for? It's funny how quick and easy you can go from feeling angry to feeling ashamed. Time to change tack. "Yeah, Ronald.

47

We're friends. Just a pair of high school buds having a reunion." I bent down, picked up Darryl's glasses, and handed them over.

"Thanks for not busting up my specs." He replaced his eyewear before looking back over to Ronnie. "I appreciate the arrival, but what I'd appreciate more right now is if you held down the fort for awhile. She and I still have a few words left unsaid."

Ronnie looked from Darryl to me to Darryl again. This was killing me, that blind faith. I wanted to tell him to run, before Darryl ran out on him.

Instead, I forced a little laugh, which came out more like *heh*. Well, I tried. "It's fine, Ronnie. We can resume our...conversation at the basketball court."

"Oh thank God!" Darryl croaked out. There was a slow creak as the gate closed behind Ronnie's departure. He tucked the gun back into his waistband and left through a far exit. Once we were alone again, Darryl fell back down to the floor of the octagon and spoke again. "So, you were really upset this whole time?"

I turned my head from the gate to the man. "How could I not be? I thought we were all gonna run off and change the world together."

"We did," Darryl said. "We did all run off and changed the world."

"Together, I said." Walking over, I sat down on the mat next to him. Careful not to sit in any blood, I propped myself up on the fence. "I expected that I'd have spent the last seven years with the five people that mattered the most to me. Doing amazing things with the path we paved as a team. Not...whatever this is." With a wave of the hand, I casually indicated our surroundings.

"I guess we...I... miscalculated. We all sort of guessed that Marcella would be hurt. But once we were able to loop you both back in at a later point in the plan, we figured it would be all forgive and forget. She's too much of a sweetheart. She couldn't stay mad at us forever. Could she?"

"That's not a completely inaccurate assessment of my girlfriend," I admitted. "But you had to know that logic wouldn't apply evenly to me."

"No. Not you." Leaning off the fence a bit, he said, "We weren't entirely sure you'd notice we were gone at all."

"What?" That stung.

"You were always so quiet. So distant. We didn't think we registered to you as friends so much as...warm, moving, useful bodies that you tolerated having around."

I laughed at that. The first real laugh I'd had all day. The first real laugh I'd had in what felt like a long while. Yeah, it was harsh, but teenaged me had been as much of a charming human being as I am to this day. Tolerate was likely exactly how it looked from the outside.

Then a thought made me go a little cold. "Mark couldn't have agreed with that analysis. He and I were dating when you all left. He had to have known that he was more than just a warm body to me. Right?" Yes, I could be single-minded and even withdrawn at times. Sarcastic.

49

Blunt. But the idea that Mark couldn't see through that to my actual feelings terrified me for an instant. My thoughts flew briefly to Marcie back in Cargill.

"He did. To be clear, Mark was enthusiastic about the plan and was determined to see its goals met, but he voted against almost every part of it that left you and Marcella out. Unfortunately, his was just one vote. Plus, the twins and I were so sure of ourselves that we convinced Mark that his objections were solely based on his relationships with you both. I guess we got that all wrong."

"Look, I *am* quiet, Darryl. I *am* distant. But that doesn't mean you weren't my best friends. It doesn't mean I would overlook your complete disappearance from my life. And, most importantly, it doesn't mean I could possibly ignore the effect it's had on Marcella...and our relationship."

Darryl gave me a long look. I wondered if he finally saw it, like Mark had. Like Marcie always could. Finally saw me. "I'm so sorry, Sana. I severely underestimated the toll all of this would take. Maybe I just deluded myself because I wanted to see the rest of the plan done. But either way, I apologize for hurting you. Both of you."

I put an arm around him and he leaned his head onto my shoulder. We stayed there like that for a few minutes. I let myself think back, to see it from his perspective. It wasn't hard to see why he thought I hadn't cared. But also, he wasn't blameless. When he said, "the plan" you could hear the unspoken "my" in it. My flaw had been my reticence, but his had always been his arrogance. We'd been stupid kids. We both believed we were right. Did it even matter now?

It felt good to connect but there was still work to be done. I eventually stood up, reached down, and helped Darryl to his feet.

As we left the cage and began in the direction of courts, I spotted a stack of clean towels. I pulled a fresh one off the top and handed it over to him. He accepted it graciously and immediately went to work mopping the blood off his swollen face. He'd heal up just fine. The nanites would sort him out by the time he got out of bed the next morning. But I still felt slightly guilty for taking out my all-too-righteous frustration on his face.

I felt like I just ran the emotional equivalent of a marathon, but there was something so good being with my friend again.

When we got to the courts, Darryl called out to the players at one section. "I need this hoop, chaps. Do you mind?" The players cringed a bit at the mess of his face.

"You alright, man?"

"What happened to your face, Frost?"

"Yo, you been in a fight?"

Darryl cheerfully replied, "Yeah. But if you think my face looks bad, you should take a look at her knuckles." They all laughed together for a moment before the players all gave their assent to the takeover of their court. They weren't mad at the interruption. They all respected

Darryl. He jogged over to the sidelines to grab a ball and to drop the towel into a laundry basket.

Once the court was clear of everyone within earshot, I couldn't stop myself from asking, "So, are you finally gonna fill me in on what's going on here, what Mark's doing in North Carolina, what are you doing in Ohio...and why are you still wearing glasses?" My head was filled with questions, but these made for a good start.

"Check!" He tossed the ball to me. "Well, I suppose I still wear the glasses for the same reason you're still a little thing. Aesthetics. With the nanites, I could've bulked up like Marcella. I could've slimmed down. I could've lost the specs. Instead, like you, I chose to stay as is and I just swapped in non-prescription lenses. And look how good we both look!" He gave both of us a glance up and down, pleased with his explanation. Pleased with himself. What else was new. "Making an exception for my present condition, of course. By the way...welcome to Phase Two."

The words sent a jolt through me. For years, they'd haunted me and it seemed like today I'd get my answers.

"Meaning what?" I took a shot. The ball landed high on the backboard then banked in. Darryl caught it and passed it back.

"Remember when we talked about the future of...our organization? I wanted to give the nanites away and you explained the drawbacks of such a plan. Well, I took it to heart. All of it. We couldn't just save the world with a solution that the people of the world hadn't earned on their own. Folks would reject it without even understanding why."

"Yeah... I remember..." I had used the pretext of correcting his vision as a chance to correct his ideas on how to use our tech as well. It was a breakthrough for our friendship. The closest I ever felt to him. A couple weeks later, he was gone. "So where did that train of thought lead you?" To avoid his eyes, I took a step further back and shot again. Nothing but net. Darryl collected the loose ball and threw it back to me.

"We decided to go slow. Methodical. Ease people into a new culture we were forming. You've been keeping up with Kani at all?"

"Not really keeping up. I'm...aware of her, though." I ground my teeth a bit at the mention of her name. Of our four missing friends, Kani Sidana was the only one Marcella and I had found when we went searching. She was the only one who wasn't really hiding.

As was her plan before we first started Team Supercell, Kani went to college to study biology. When Marcella and I confronted her at her school, she barely acknowledged us. She just told us that she had other plans for her life and blew us off. It was especially hard on Marcie. She and Kani weren't in love or anything, but they were close and had been intimate several times. To be treated like an annoyance by someone who was, up until recently, a valued friend was crushing. It kept us from searching harder for the rest of the team. After a year or two, we stopped altogether. We didn't think we'd like what we'd find anyway.

Darryl saw the look on my face. "She's sorry about what happened, y'know," he said softly. "She had to direct you elsewhere. She probably felt as terrible about it as you did."

"I doubt that." As I'd had to console a sobbing Marcie for a week straight afterward, I wasn't ready to accept Kani's struggle or this third-hand apology. Another shot, another make. This time the ball bounced back over to me.

"Well, we needed her at university and there was no way to hide her there. So, we agreed that, if confronted, she would dismiss you both. If only to deter you from looking for the rest of us. Hardest thing she's ever had to do."

I was done hearing about our dismissal...and Kani's pain. I took another shot and pushed ahead. "Why'd you need her in college while the rest of you hid?" The shot clanged loudly off the rim and out of bounds. Darryl kept talking as he went to retrieve the ball.

"The rest of our roles relied solely on what we could do. Kani's required credentials. She couldn't be the nation's premier voice on healthcare matters without first being a doctor. With her Supercell-enhanced intelligence, she tested out of her courses so fast it made her professors' heads spin. With her alternate take on human biology, based on her Supercell research, she's been providing nonstop medical breakthroughs for the last three years."

When I said I was aware of Kani, I meant I'd seen her on TV appearances, newspaper clippings, and social media feeds. I often changed the channel or hid the media from Marcella. But I still only had a vague idea of what she was doing in terms of her day-to-day. "So, you're giving the people Supercell results...without giving them Supercell technology?"

"Kinda sorta, yeah. It's not nanites but it's steadily improving health conditions nationwide." He took and made a shot before collecting his own stray ball.

"Kazi popped up on our radar as well." A few years after his disappearance, Marcie and I spotted Kani's twin brother, Kazi, on television revealing a new video game at some major geek convention. We had money and connections at that point. We could've flown there by the end of the event. I'd asked her if she wanted to go and maybe confront him. She'd just left the room.

"Yeah...he started out Phase Two right here in this rec center. While I was building the team of hackers you saw earlier, Kazi kept busy making fun and popular strategy games for mobile phones. The catch is that they low-key mimicked perfectly functioning military defense grids. Eventually, the government contracted him to make the real thing. His development studio was the best possible cover. He hid in plain sight after that and they basically gave him the keys to the castle. Keys that he made a copy of for me."

"So, now you've got a hand in both health and national security matters?"

"I assume you researched on the way over here what Mark is doing and where he's located? If you did, then you know..." he held out a hand to indicate that I should finish his sentence.

"Then I know he's priming himself for a major political run as soon as he hits the age requirements."

"Exactly! When is a coup not a coup?" Darryl shot again, made it, but still tossed me the ball as if he had missed.

"When no one knows it's even happening. How do you fit in? And how do I?"

"Aside from being the man with the plan? You and I have essentially the same role. When someone stands a chance of derailing Mark or Kani or Kazi, Mr. Frost gets in the way. Sometimes, that means digging up enough dirt to fluster or delay a political opponent. Sometimes that means adding a mild virus to a competitor's dev servers. Sometimes that means sending an operator to intimidate an elected official into adding some healthcare funding to their local budget." He raised an eyebrow at me for the last one. It was a job I did for him eighteen months ago.

I put the ball on my hip and stood up straight. I mentally reviewed job after job and came up with the same result. "So wait...has every contract I've taken for you been towards this same effort?"

"Pretty much, yeah. I only ever needed an operator in certain situations and I only ever contracted you in those situations."

"Well, that's bullshit. You should've just told us! I was already part of the team. I would've willingly been part of the process. We both would've. Me in the same role I already occupied. Marcella as a popular and public facing superhero."

"Of course you would've been part of the process. But you told me to find a way to help that made sense to me. It wasn't fair to disrupt the way that made sense to you."

"Maybe," I said between gritted teeth. As much as I wanted to, I couldn't let myself get sidetracked by what ifs. "We gave you the fucking means, Darryl." I threw the ball at him. He barely caught it before it slammed into his stomach. "The capital that probably launched this rec center and this whole movement of yours? The nanites that made all your brilliant strategies possible? That was all me and Marcie. We brought you into our project. And then you all bolted to start your own initiative without so much as an invitation. Without an explanation. With only a single note as a goodbye. We didn't deserve that. We didn't deserve having our tech stolen by our friends. We didn't deserve having Kani treat us like garbage. You owed us at least the chance to hear your ideas and to make informed decisions."

"That's what Mark said. I wasn't too sure. We didn't steal your tech, though. We earned it. It was the agreed-upon payment for designing the app I assume you're both still using. And the money you gave all of us came from a budget surplus that you only had because Kani's ideas drastically reduced your development costs. Technically speaking, we didn't owe you anything." He ignored my skeptical look. "But it was ultimately my call to leave you in the dark. The twins were uneasy with it, but they voted my way. To keep you two uninvolved until it was absolutely time to bring you in. We got it wrong. You deserved more regard than we gave you. Again...I'm sorry. But I fear the moment for your direct involvement has arrived." He began casually dribbling again. Moving along the three-point line and looking for a shot.

"Why now? What's changed?"

"So... you called to my attention how many multi-billion-dollar industries we could potentially shut down. How that would endanger us? Well, what if it's not about money, but about power and control of an entire nation?" He stepped out of his shooting motion and looked me directly in the eyes. "It was all well and good when we were playing the game against businesses, and bureaucrats, and their lobbyists. The initial plan was to eventually ask you and Marcella to be our public faces. Political advocates. As superheroes, your expected level of popularity would give us lots of pull with the masses. Active and visible influence. But that wouldn't have been for another three years. Far earlier than we predicted, active became more important than visible. We needed an operator. Mark knew you well enough to think you might struggle playing the hero. But it was my idea to offer you your first contract."

"Thus manipulating me further into a game plan you didn't make me aware of while simultaneously triggering the strain that's had me and Marcie walking on eggshells for the last five years or so. Thanks for that."

"That's on you. Look, I'm beginning to understand the damage we've done. Abandoning you was shitty. Clearly. But you didn't have to take that contract. You could've deleted that email. You could've deleted them all. I made you an offer. And instead of remaining by your girlfriend's side as a superhero, you chose me. You chose me!

"We didn't mean to exploit you. It was a win for both of us. We got the help we needed, and you got a new life that made more sense than the hero one you were living. A new life you appear to have greatly enjoyed, by the way. I'm not saying we went about this the right way. Just that your choices factored in as well. Plus, we all figured that if any superhero/operator combo could make it work, it'd be you two. And here you are...still together."

I had to work to unclench my jaw. "Fine. You've made your point. Tell me the rest of it. You jumped me into Phase Two early and on the low. Now you're jumping me in even further out in the open. Why?"

"There's something more involved here. A higher class of villainy afoot. An end boss we hadn't anticipated."

"You're talking about something above the political elite?"

"Right. And as soon as Mark wins this election—and he will— the eyes of our opponent will be firmly fixed in our direction. We need you to blind those eyes...to kill that opponent."

"For the fifteenth goddamn time, what's changed? You could've reached out to 'JC' and contracted my help."

"We need you to go full time, now. No other clients. No more contracts. No more downtime between jobs. The landscape has changed and it's kind of hard to explain, but...is there any chance that you believe in magic?"

"Oh, for fuck's sake!"

Chapter Six

"The only thing really surprising about the acceptance of extralegal operations is who led the charge at the end. Back when they were still calling it 'legal dirty work,' politicians Dale Roberts and Chris Hanney inexplicably changed their stances. They both went from being loud opponents to fierce advocates almost overnight. I have no doubt that it would've been voted into law regardless. But that shift in politics sealed the deal."

— *Dr. Carly Steif in* For Hire *magazine — April 1991*

A few minutes later we were back in Darryl's command center. Ha! He literally called it a "command center." Once a dork, always a dork. He needed me to see and understand the exact reason JC was going full time. When we entered the room, I watched as he ordered his team of hackers to find a logical closure point for their work and then to call it a night. Some left almost immediately, others slowly wrapped up their projects and filtered out at their own pace. Either way, Darryl wasn't waiting to be alone.

He took up the same workstation he occupied when I first got here and logged in. It took only a glance to realize that this wasn't a random choice. This was his workstation. There were several collectibles and action figures of various styles posed around the desk, including three different versions of Double M. A scattered assortment of photos were thumbtacked to the wall. They appeared to be of Darryl with several of the kids here at this center. There was always a pool or a court in the background. It must have been years' worth of shots, as there was even one of him helping a much-younger Ronnie. Darryl was putting a bandage over Ronnie's freshly skinned knee.

I realized what I was looking for wasn't on the wall but framed. It was us, the six of us on the night when we'd finished development on Supercell. Marcella and I had ingested the nanites that day. And though the rest of the team would wait until they saw our results before following suit, Kazi had still suggested that we go out to dinner together to celebrate the project's completion. We ate and laughed and discussed our future. We knew our worlds were about to change.

M and I had thought we'd known how. But then there was that empty lab, and the note, and seven years without closure.

I thought about the prospect of this photo outing me and Double M to the rest of Darryl's team. Ultimately, I dismissed the concern. Double M was huge and ripped now, a modern-day Greek goddess chiseled out of marble. The Marcella McKenzie in this seven-year-old picture was tall and gangly with violently orange hair in place of her current trademark dark purple. Her smile was the same: big and beautiful. It had only been a day and I was already missing it. Even next to toys based on her future likeness, the girl in the photo was unrecognizable.

As for me, I looked roughly the same. My hair was styled differently; pulled back in a thick ponytail now as opposed to the lovely crown of natural brown curls I used to wear. But that was about it. I was literally a single hair tie away from being that eighteen-year-old girl again. I'd be easy to recognize if I wasn't hiding in the background behind my partners, Marcella and Mark, with their larger-than-life, charismatic personalities. Felt symbolic. My mother took this picture, I remembered, as I caught glimpses of her in my own face. I made a mental note to call her.

Pulling out of the brief reverie, I rolled an empty chair next to Darryl's own, sat down, and whipped out my tablet. I logged in and cleared out the notes from my op earlier this evening. No use for them now. I fired up my research app. Darryl wanted to take me on a journey and I meant to follow along closely.

"Alright, love! I know you're brilliant at researching, so tell me about Quietus. The pharma company. What's the deal with their funding?"

With a raised eyebrow, I decided to humor the man. Their systems weren't protected particularly well, so I was able to access their financial records and cross-check what I found against media reports and the company's own public-facing website. It didn't take long to spot the discrepancy. "Their funding is solid. Nothing private or shady. It's just a steady stream of government capital straight from the taxpayers direct to their coffers. But here's the clincher: They don't make anything. They're a pharmaceutical company but I don't see a single drug that they've ever delivered to market. Every penny goes directly to research and development...which would be fine except that I also don't see an employment roster. No CEO. No CFO. No chemists. I don't even see a janitor. For that matter, the place doesn't even have an address."

"Oh really?" Darryl said with a smirk that might've passed for charming on a face that wasn't so swollen. "Well, if they don't have the trappings of a legit business, how did they secure that funding?"

I was already halfway into finding the answer as he was asking the question. "Okay, so this doesn't make sense. Congressman Elliott Vann worked to get funding diverted to Quietus from the previous contract holders at Frowley Creations. But Vann was skimming money from Frowley. I remember this story. Vann was eventually indicted for this. He's in prison now. He leveraged his political power to get taxpayer dollars for Frowley and then siphoned off a big chunk of it into his own pockets. Why would he shut off his own faucet?"

"Why indeed? And imagine the precise timing that allowed for Vann to push the budget consideration to Quietus only days before he got caught taking money from Frowley."

"So fuck Vann but what happened to Frowley? Their employees, their products?"

"They shut down. The scandal broke them. And without the life-saving meds they were producing, their competitors jacked up their own prices citing the burden of increased production."

"Riiiight," I said. "This is what you do here though. Isn't it? Ronnie says you recover money lost due to waste, fraud, and abuse."

"That is what we do here. On a normal day, me or one of my associates would've exposed the thirty thousand that Vann was skimming from Frowley each month. We'd pocket three thou for ourselves, as a leech removal fee, then return the rest to Frowley's budget. But in this case, Vann moved the money just before he was exposed by an anonymous whistleblower. When we checked out Quietus, we found what you found. But with no way to prove waste, fraud, or abuse, there was nothing we could do about it. The company is a fake but it's still a money pit. Somebody is collecting. But no one knows who."

"Can't you...I don't know...report the existence of this fake company as a whole?" This had been my fight for all of ten minutes and I was already frustrated by the lack of progress.

"At that level, there isn't anyone to report to. Not without exposing ourselves here. Quietus isn't the first of these I've encountered. Check out Sahar Natal's voting record. Particular when it comes to military spending." He sat back in his chair and put his feet up on the nearest desk.

I was enthralled by the challenge of this mystery now. My fingers were a blur across the keys. It didn't take long to look up the honorable representative's record. Natal had voted consistently for reduced military spending. Until she didn't. "I don't get it. She only voted for increased spending once. When she did it was for a colossal expansion. The largest budget surge in decades."

Darryl brought his feet down and began typing furiously at his own workstation. "Keep going. Tell me more."

"Not only did Natal vote against her usual record and against her party...but she was the deciding swing vote. This bump couldn't have happened without her. It doesn't make any sense. But I guess politicians waffle all the time."

"That they do, love. That they do." With that, Darryl pointed to his monitors. I leaned in and looked at both. On the left were articles documenting Natal's fight against colonialism. Not just a voting record, but interviews, campaign speeches, the bullet points on her website. It was her entire platform. She was a die-hard...except for this singular vote. On the right monitor was what appeared to be personal text messages to an unknown party.

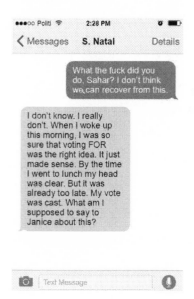

Unknown: What the fuck did you do, Sahar? I don't think we can recover from this.
Natal: I don't know. I really don't. When I woke up this morning, I was so sure that voting FOR was the right idea. It just made sense. By the time I went to lunch my head was clear. But it was already too late. My vote was cast. What am I supposed to say to Janice about this?

"So... how? Was she drugged? Hypnotized? She changed her opinion for a few hours just in time for the biggest possible vote against her own interests? This isn't a coincidence."

"No one said it was. Follow the money! Who won out the most with this new budget?"

I started comparing budgets from year-to-year. Line item by line item. Endowment by endowment. Most beneficiaries of the new budget gained or lost a percentage point or two. Unquestionably, the highest amount of movement went to a defense contractor called Proxima. Proxima had just appeared out of nowhere and was immediately granted a budget surpassing longstanding and long-trusted merchants. Following the same methodology for my research into Quietus, I checked for a staff roster. Nothing. I checked for an address. Nothing. I checked for a client list. Nothing. "What the fuck is this, Frost? What are Quietus and Proxima? Where is this money going?"

"Where indeed, Ms. Clementine." At this point, Darryl was smiling broadly. Clearly, this little exercise had produced the results he was looking for.

"Stop grinning at me and explain this shit!" Suddenly, the operator who stringently avoided the narrative was knee-deep in it again.

"Okay. To backtrack, Phase Two of our plan started with me piercing the inner workings of government and medicine and finance and the military. My end was to figure out the most strategic places for us to strike. For the most part, it was smooth sailing. But then I'd start hitting these dead-ends. These politicians were acting against themselves incomprehensibly, handing money, power, and authority to organizations with no address. Bank accounts that don't exist."

"And nobody spotted this? A journalist should've picked up on this."

"The details aren't what sell newspapers, commercials, and banner ad space. The headline is Vann being exposed for taking money or Natal supporting the military industrial complex. The sexy story is the resulting damage to both of their careers. Meanwhile, the beneficiaries of these decisions are far enough down the chain that they get lost in the sauce. The individual purchases of these beneficiaries or lack thereof go completely unnoticed."

"So, who's at the top of this?"

Darryl threw up his hands. "I don't know. It's amazingly subtle. I know how to follow the influence from specific choices all the way back to power gained. The circumstances are too varied though." He opened a window with a digital workspace that resembled a conspiracy theorist's wet dream. Dozens of photos of politicians. Each connected with colored lines to screenshots of social media entries, text entries of bank account numbers, and images of various buildings. He waved his hand across the entire display. "If it's drugging, it can't be drugging for all of them. If it's hypnosis, it can't be hypnosis for all of them. Whatever they're doing to all these influencers, the results are exactly the same. But there's no known method of enthralling people that can be even applied to everyone we believe to have been manipulated."

"And you think this is the work of more than one person?"

"There's never more than a small amount of these occurrences happening at once. Without knowing the method, for sure, it's hard to tell. I've narrowed it down to less than five culprits. Less than five but more than one. I can tell you all the details but not the who or the how. It's inexplicable. As much as I hate leaning into the unknown, the fact is when you rule out the impossible, the only thing that could explain it all is magic."

Suddenly, I was sixteen years old again, eating a bowl of cereal with my feet in Marcella's lap and arguing about whether the Amazing Magisteria's shows were real or not. "If you rule out the impossible, the only thing that can explain it all...is magic," she'd told me, eyes wide with joy and wonder. It was the only proof she needed to believe in magic. I'd rolled my eyes, maybe called her cheesy or gullible. Even after all this time, she was the dreamer, and I was the cynic. Except now I'd seen proof.

I put my head in my hands. This was going to get worse before it got better. "Look, I think I know someone I can talk to. We can figure this out."

Darryl pumped his fists in response. "I knew you'd have something! You're the top op, after all. So you're in then? Really and truly?"

My first thought was what an operation like this could do for my girl. As Double M, she'd been fighting to create opportunities. More stable living conditions. A better world. This was a chance to get a very real barrier out of the way. I had to take this. "Really and truly," I said. "But I've got to speak to Marcella first."

"You mean to check in, la la la, just another day on the job, darling, see you soon, right? I need you to get to this contact yesterday."

"You mean instead of saying 'Hey, Marcie, I found our missing friends'?" We locked eyes. "'Turns out they were just really dense'?"

"Sana, you can't tell her about this yet."

I stood up and grabbed him by the front of his shirt. "I am **not** going to be another person lying to her, do you understand me, Darryl?"

He put his hands up over his bruised face. It already looked suspiciously better. How did he pass that off to his staff? GVS? "You're right. You're right. You're right. But please listen! Right now, whoever this is that we're after? They don't know we exist. They believe themselves unopposed. They have been for decades as far as I can tell. We can only operate against them from the shadows until Mark wins his election. Frankly, I think we'll need every second of that lead time. If you put Marcella on the board, it exposes us immediately. She's got all the subtlety of a wrench to the face."

I unclenched my fist and the fabric fell, wrinkled, back into place. He wasn't wrong. That was Double M in a nutshell. Even if the job required a sniper rifle, she would show up with a rocket launcher. It's what made her such a successful hero. "Look...I'm leaving. This was a lot and I understand what the stakes are. But this requires more tech and more planning than I've got available right now anyway. So, do whatever it is that you do here. I'm going to go home and get the rest of my gear. I won't tell her about all of this, but my girlfriend is not gonna think I was killed in action or that I just disappeared on her. Not like the rest of you. We can work out the rest of the details after that." With that, I turned and left, all the goodwill from my nostalgia effectively drained.

I had a seat on the next flight to Cargill booked before I hit the rec center doors.

Chapter Seven

"Double M had been number one in the rankings for a year and I was just behind her at number two for months. I know it's not supposed to be a competition. I know we're all fighting the good fight. But I was envious of her position. I used to complain about it to my friends. Then out of the blue, I get a phone call from her. She said she's gonna be in town, she's a fan of my work, and she wants to meet me. M shows up in Miami a week later and takes me out to dinner at my favorite spot. I thought, in person, I was gonna see right through her act. I'm embarrassed by how wrong I was. She was charming. She was hilarious. She was genuine. Then after way too many drinks, she asked if we could go out on patrol together. I was drunk, but I wasn't gonna say no. Not in my own city. Somehow, she was still sharp and, without ever mentioning it, she just compensated for every move I was too tipsy to make. It was like we were longtime partners. We brought down a trafficking ring that night. And I got to see why she was number one, first hand. I never complained about her again. Instead I worked harder to be like her."
— *Miami-based superhero Navara* — For Hire *magazine* — *March 2017*

I wasn't nervous about the job, or rather the upcoming series of jobs that my new life was about to consist of. I wasn't even scared of all the new information I received while Ronnie brought me back to the airport for my return flight. The thing that really rattled me was how little I'd be able to relay to Marcella. As always, she was central to my thoughts.

After all my rage at Darryl, it made me feel like a hypocrite to side with him, but he knew what he was talking about, both when it came to the job and when it came to Double M. Kani and Kazi's indirect involvement in government matters could be overlooked. As a pair of brilliant twins, perhaps they were both just destined for an equal measure of greatness. But the people we were up against weren't dumb. They were powerful and formidable and undoubtedly as clued into the landscape as we were.

A third person from the same Rhodes High School graduating class, charging hard towards political power from a strategically perfect yet seemingly insignificant small town? Those were dots begging to be connected. Mark's rise would be a signal to the enemy that a second group of players were in the game. Putting the country's most famous superhero in the mix—a woman of the same age and from a neighboring small town—wouldn't be a signal. It would be a bright, shining beacon from a snow-covered mountaintop. She had to be kept in the dark.

So now I'd joined the majority membership of Team Supercell in their secret agenda, yet one more person deciding what Marcella should and shouldn't know about circumstances that affect her, yet one more friend being untruthful to her. Not just avoiding difficult truths, but actively deceiving her, the person I care the most about. Shit, maybe

I should at least let her know that much, since I was about to be lying about basically everything else.

As angry as I was when I got to Columbus, a lot of what happened once I got there was pleasantly familiar. Shooting around. Solving problems collaboratively with Darryl. Laughing a bit. I wondered if the rest of the team maintained the same carefree energy we had when we were all together. That feeling that we'd be on summer break for the rest of our lives. I'd tapped into that energy again tonight for the first time in years. It felt good...and I was heading home now to deny that opportunity to my girl. Ugh.

The flight felt like it took forever, my stomach sinking with the descent of the plane. It was late when I got back to Cargill, roundabouts two in the morning. The traffic was light but so was the availability of taxi cabs from the airport. When I finally got to our apartment, I found Marcella awake in bed, reading from her tablet and wearing a tank top with my favorite pajama bottoms. I liked them long enough to brush lightly against my toes and baggy enough to fit my armor underneath on nights when I was feeling paranoid, but they fit her the way they were meant to. She was sandwiched between a pair of sleeping men. Both were naked and covered in fresh red welts; one still wore a handcuff on his right wrist. She spotted me in the bedroom doorway and quietly slipped out from between them. She wiggled straight down to the foot of the bed and hopped off the edge with a light skip that defied her size.

"Hey," she said in a hushed tone, coming out to the living room. "I wasn't sure you were coming in tonight."

There was too much physical distance between us. She didn't hug or kiss me when she got near. The worst was that she didn't smile when she saw me. I really could've used a smile from her tonight.

"Yeah, things haven't really gone the way I expected since I left. How was your training session? Are those your new trainees?" Babbling, putting off the inevitable. I was a coward.

She gave me The Look. Already. I was stumbling out of the gate. "You know I don't fuck my trainees. Or at least you *should* know that. That would be improper due to the power dynamics of our relationship. Those two are just a couple of friends from the local force. You've met them both before at least twice. If I knew you were coming home, I probably would've encouraged them to head out earlier. Probably. How was the trip?"

"Like I said, it went in a direction I couldn't have anticipated. It's got me a little rattled." This was normally the point where she'd hug me. She'd make sure I was okay. She'd offer support. Nothing.

"Did you finish what you started? Is your spot on the power rankings secure?" She'd never asked me about the rankings before. She'd congratulated me when I hit the top ten and again when I hit number one, but those were both short, tensely-worded compliments. Now that she had mentioned it, I did wonder whether Darryl had marked my contract fulfilled. I hadn't checked my email since leaving Raleigh International.

"That's not really what I need to talk about." I took a deep breath. "I'm gonna be a bit hard to reach for a while. The job that I worked yesterday has taken a sort of turn. The scope has exceeded the boundaries of the original contract by a considerable degree. The next part...the next few parts are gonna require me to go dark. I don't know for how long. I came home tonight to get all my on-the-job gear." I was not just going to disappear from her life. She had to know that. "I just want you to know that I love you. You're the most important part of my life."

"Well, that's ominous."

"I don't mean it like that. I just don't want you taking my absence to mean that I don't care. I just—"

"Ha!" She tossed her hair back over her shoulder. That was a classic Double M intimidation move. It was even in the licensed video game. "You think your absence is going to make me question whether you care, Sana? No. Your *presence* makes me question whether you care. You choosing a job that takes you away the day after we fight makes me question whether you care."

I was finally starting to get that the usual script was out the window. She was hurting, deep, and I didn't have the first clue as to how to fix that. I'd never been the nurturing one. My role was limited to mostly saying *You'll get that asshole next time* or *She/he/they weren't good enough for you anyway.*

"Look, this isn't great timing, I get that. I wouldn't have taken a job away if it wasn't important. The last twelve hours or so have given me some perspective. About you and me and us. I just can't do anything with that perspective until this contract wraps."

75

She stared at me coldly for what felt like a full minute. "Twelve hours? Okay, I'll bite. Tell me about this new perspective."

"I can't." I lowered my head. "Not now."

She just pursed her lips and kept staring down at me. "Okay," she said, taking a deep breath and letting it out slowly." Tell me about this contract. Where did you go this afternoon? What changed between then and now?"

"I... I can't, Marcella."

"You won't. This isn't about contract terms, or power rankings, or expanded mission parameters, Sana. This is about choices. And you're making one. So, I'm making one too." I misread her end of this conversation several times. But I knew where she was headed this time for sure.

"Marce...please don't. I need you. I need you to be here when I get back." Amazing how quickly you can go from feeling like an action hero to being a woman on the edge of falling apart. Twelve hours might be a record.

"I can't really promise that, Sa. I don't know if this is sustainable for me anymore. Do whatever it is you need to do. Call me when it's done. Maybe I'll answer. In the meantime, get your gear or whatever and get the fuck out of here." She leaned in and gave me the most passionless kiss I could imagine but no goodbye as she left the room. I wanted to explain it to her honestly. I wanted to tell her about everything that'd occurred from the moment Voss walked into the pub all the way up to now. But she was right about me. Darryl was too. I was making a choice and, if I was making that choice, there was nothing left to say. This was on me.

Marce woke up the guys in our—her bed and sent them away. I avoided their looks by heading to the vacant bedroom we used as a storeroom and design studio. I grabbed a large backpack. Hers. But fuck it. I packed up the remainder of my gear: weaponry, a prototype of modular armor, my laptop, a tool kit, and two flash drives full of contacts and unfinished designs. I had no idea if I'd need any of these but being over-prepared is kinda my thing.

By the time I finished in the studio, Marcella's friends were gone and she was in the bathroom with the shower running. She never kept her nanite-enhanced hearing as dialed up as I did. Her job didn't require it like mine did. So she thought the sound of the running water could mask the fact that she was really just sitting in the bathroom sobbing. I couldn't bear it. Her crying made me start crying. I grabbed the rolling suitcase that I arrived with and moved quickly to the bedroom. There, I packed a few changes of clothes. Then I made a beeline to the door with my bags and left the apartment for what I hoped wouldn't be the last time.

Chapter Eight

"It was just a coincidence. I was getting lunch at the food truck in front of For Hire's *offices when I heard a series of booms. They sounded like thunderclaps getting closer. Next thing you know, they were right on the street near me. It was Double M and Cobb, the former hero. They were throwing down. Cobb might be a little older but he's crafty and seriously strong. I've been a writer for this magazine for M's whole career and I've never heard of her taking the kind of pounding she took that day. She won though. She was roughed up pretty badly, but she won. That's not the strange part. Word is that M visited Cobb in prison after they finally had him locked away. Less than an hour later, the crowd fund for Cobb's daughter's medical bills were paid in full. That fund had been stagnant for months. It's the reason Cobb started robbing banks in the first place. Then, out of nowhere, an anonymous six figure payment. We don't deserve her, man. We really don't."*

— *Mitch Tisdale, writer for* For Hire *magazine* — *February 2016*

I was back in Luke's Lockup just before last call. I had nowhere else to go. It was too late to even check into a hotel. Not on a weekend in a busy city like Cargill. Everywhere that wasn't a rat warren was already booked solid. Had the shoe been on the other foot, Marce would have had a dozen friends lined up offering her a place to stay tonight. Hell, had the shoe been on the other foot, she'd have just come back home and curled up in bed with me again, trusting that we'd both be less mad in the morning than we were when we went to sleep. I didn't have the confidence to pull off that bold of a move. I knew that, and she knew that. But, knowing her, she was sitting in bed waiting for me to try anyway...but understanding that I wouldn't. I'd always been better with tech than with people.

So, with no local friends to turn to, I drowned my sorrows in beer. I didn't remember the name, but it was the same Australian brand that Voss brought me the other day. Except I meant to finish this mug. Voss. If I had their number, I'd call them. Maybe see if they had a place I could crash for the night. I had to find a way to talk to them about magic for the next phase of this operation, and yet there I was thinking about them as a measure of support. Just that thought was funny enough to make me laugh through the tears. Or maybe that was the beer talking.

Then Marcella appeared. This was the second time in just a few days that I'd had an unexpected run-in with her while sitting in this very booth. Last time was the forgotten magazine. This time it was her most recent talk show appearance. Late night host Shae Livingston had her in the studio about a week and a half prior. I forgot that the interview was supposed to air hours ago, around the same time I was back in Columbus sorting things out with Darryl. This must be one of those dead-time entertainment shows that just replayed popular clips with new commentary.

Either way, it made me feel even worse about the current situation. Had I been home and off the clock, Marce and I probably would've watched the show together. She wouldn't have needed to call in those two guys she was with. Or maybe she still would've called them over. We could've have enjoyed the show and the guys together. Meanwhile, at the pub, I couldn't even enjoy the show. Besides my current mood, the television was on the far side of the room, all the way behind the bar. I couldn't even hear what was being said. The other patrons were loving it though. Smiles. Laughter. Edge-of-their-seat attention. That's the kind of audience she commanded. I wanted to leave.

The next flight back to Columbus wasn't until after sunrise. All I could do was sit there in misery until it was time to head to the airport. There were several hours between when Luke's closed and when the flight left. I guess I'd be sleeping it off spread out across several seats at the departure gate. In the meantime, I killed the rest of my drink and ordered another. I had to get good and trashed before last call and the recovery powers of my nanites didn't really make that easy. Maybe I should've been ordering shots. Action hero, indeed.

By the time my head became clear again, it was 10 in the morning and I was crawling out of a cab in Ohio. I barely remembered getting there from the airport. I barely remembered getting from Luke's to the airport back home. Sometimes, alcohol is its own superpower. Time travel, maybe...or teleportation...or both. The rec center was far quieter than it had been last night. The pool and the exercise facilities were in use. I could hear instructors from both shouting orders to some morning class attendees. The distinctive sounds that mark the use of the basketball courts and what I've come to call "the combat room" were nonexistent.

There'd clearly been a shift change since overnight. I didn't recognize any of the staff as I walked in. Everyone was still very friendly. Excessively so, given the hour. Annoyingly so. People who were that chipper before noon should be locked up. It almost felt like this was a hotel or a restaurant and the staff were all determined to make sure that I enjoyed my stay.

That level of warmth might have made sense for long-time club goers who had an established level of familiarity with the people who worked there, people they saw regularly. But I wasn't a member and those employees didn't know me. Even still, no one attempted to stop me as I dragged myself and my bags through the doors leading to the computer stations. It's entirely possible that I just didn't remember calling ahead or sending a message to the Frost client ID to indicate my arrival. There's no way they'd just allow me or anybody else back there if it represented a security breach.

When I arrived at the command center, there were only three people on hand. Two early bird hackers typed away furiously. I vaguely recognized them as a pair who had left with Frost's early dismissal. They were likely back there to complete whatever task they had left unfinished the night before. And, of course, Mr. Frost himself was back at it. "Did you even sleep at all?" I said as I approached him.

"I did, indeed, my dear Ms. Clementine. But it looks clear that you have not. Or, if you did sleep, you didn't sleep very well. How did last night go? How'd she take it?" He rolled his chair away from his desk and looked at me.

"I don't want to talk about that. Not now and not with you. Do you have a place where I can put my stuff?" The concern was appreciated but not the familiar tone. Not when I'd gotten my heart stepped on because of his stupid Phase Two.

"Yeah. I've got you covered," He pushed off and rolled his chair in a backwards glide to a blank wall on the far end of the room. When he got to the wall, he placed his hand on a smooth panel. "Over here is a touchpad that reveals a lift. The lift goes up just one floor to a dorm area. It was meant for the crew here, in case anyone needed a place to stay or a quick nap mid-task. But the money we make here is good. After a week or two on the job, my people can afford apartments or homes. They can afford cars or cab rides back to those apartments or homes. So, the comfy dorms I had installed go mostly unused. The only person who stays here overnight is me. Or sometimes Ronnie when I'm away on other business. Would you like me to show you around?"

"No. But thank you. I'll manage. I'll be back down soon. We gotta get started." I stepped on the elevator and pressed the only button available. There was also a small monitor with a speaker, but I had no interest in who it was used to speak to.

The doors shut momentarily before reopening on the next floor. It was as comfy as Darryl said it would be. To the left of the elevator

82

there was a common area with a couch, several smaller chairs, and a mounted television attached to two video game consoles. Just below that was a rack of games and movies. I immediately felt at home in that space and assumed I'd be spending a chunk of any available downtime right there in that room. Over to the right of the elevator was a kitchenette. Functional, but nothing to really write home about.

Straight ahead, past the common area, was a group of six full-sized beds. All placed symmetrically and equidistant. Six seemed an odd number of beds until I recognized the bedsheets and the nightstands. Then I realized why the common area felt so welcoming to me. The sheets and bedside tables were the same style from my bedroom growing up back in New Jersey. The common area was arranged the way my mother's living room was set up back when I still lived there. Frost deliberately borrowed elements from my childhood. Was this a trick? Something to draw me in further? No. This dorm was built several years ago. The sheets were slightly worn. This wasn't made for me. It was made by Darryl and for him as well. The time we spent making Supercell had been full of days where the six of us camped out in that living room playing video games and making big plans. When development went into crunch time, each member of the team spent at least a little time napping in my bed or on that couch in between shifts. Darryl wanted to recreate that feeling for a group of young hackers that would never know the origin story behind the décor. They barely ever stayed in that place. They'd have never been able to appreciate it the way I did. Damn shame.

I spotted what looked to be the bathroom just beyond the sleeping area. I chose a bed at random and left my luggage there. When I got to the restroom facilities, I was mildly disappointed to find that they were just generic toilets, sinks, and showers. I halfway expected to find bath mats from my childhood or my favorite brand of toothpaste or something. Either way, it was a fine layout and I expected that I wouldn't complain about staying there while I did everything that needed to be done next.

First, though, a shower.

When I got back down to the command center, a few more seats had filled among the workstations. I sat my backpack down and plopped into a chair next to Darryl, who had just started watching a video from a clip sharing site. It was last night's episode of the Shae Livingston Show. "I meant to watch this when it aired," Darryl said. He could tell I was uncomfortable. "I can turn it off if you like."

"It's fine. I meant to watch it too. It was recorded about a week ago. I think it's just her talking about the training program she's trying to get moving." I had to get used to viewing Marcella the way the rest of the world does: from a distance, as a fan.

As the clip opened, a young black woman sat behind a desk wearing a sharp suit, short natural hair, and a huge smile. Shae Livingston, a comedian turned actress turned host of the most popular late-night show running, addressed her studio audience. "Tonight!" she called out to the crowd, whose applause and cheering never seemed to end. "We've got a special treat for you. Returning for her fourth appearance, *For Hire*'s number one superhero for TWENTY! SEVEN! MONTHS! STRAIGHT! The lovely! The invincible! Double M!"

Marcella came striding out from backstage. All hair, smiles, and confidence. She blew a kiss to the in-studio band and waved to her legion of fans. She wore a short but flowy dress of blue, pink, and purple sequins. I was just thinking about how she looked like a disco ball when she paused to do a twirl just before she got to her seat, the sequins hitting the light exactly as I thought they would. I did not recognize that dress. She sat down, took a breath, and waited for the applause to die down. That took a while. Then she smirked at the host and said, "Invincible, Shae? Lovely, sure. But invincible's a bit much. Don't you think that's a bit much?" she asked the audience, who roared.

Livingston threw a hand to her chest in mock outrage, "Never, and I'll keep saying it. I'm waiting on someone to prove me wrong."

"Are you?" Double M replied in a mock serious tone. "Is that what you're waiting for? You want someone to prove you wrong? Just when you think you're friends with a talk show host, you find out they're plotting your downfall."

"Oh I'm so sorry," Livingston said, embarrassed, thrown off her game in a way that made me grin. Not many got it over on Shae Livingston. "I just meant..."

"It's fine, Shae. It's fine. I'm an excellent investigator and I've been on this show many times. I know how you do me. I already knew that if I got a knife in the back, it would be your hand on the grip." The two friends shared a laugh with the audience before M continued, "But if I did get taken down, presumably by you in a fit of jealous rage, I'd like to think there were a few young heroes who might show up to avenge me."

Livingston's eyes went wide. She was still half laughing at the jealousy crack when she struggled to catch her breath. "Waitaminute! Did you? Did you just segue my audience? Did you just come on to my show, sit in my chair, and do my job for me?"

At that, Double M reached over and took a delicate sip out of Livingston's cup, even holding it like the host would. All to thunderous applause. "With all this talk of you murdering me, one of us had to get to the point, right?" She said the last bit with an exaggerated hair flip.

The audience loved it. These two always played off each other perfectly. Early in our respective careers, before I even broke into the Top 25 for Operators, I had attended Marcella's first appearance on the show. I sat way in the back and laughed my ass off. The two of them had such a strong onstage dynamic that they quickly became pals offstage as well. Marcie was good for that sort of thing. Fast friends wherever she went.

"Well, I guess I better tell my agent to stop delaying negotiations for my contract extension. I don't want the producers to get any bright ideas about replacing me here." The two laughed at the thought, but Double M would be great on this kind of show. Too bad she'd be bored to tears within two weeks. "So, tell me about these young heroes. You're building a small army, correct?"

"Kinda sorta but no, not really. See, the superhero culture is hyper-competitive. When I first got started as a hero, a lot of the active leaders on the power rankings were really hard on me. I don't know if it was my age, or my talents, or my hair. But a lot of the top dogs just didn't like me." The crowd began to boo and Marce held up her hands. "No, no, no. It's okay. It's fine. Times are hard, and we've got a stressful job. These were all brave and honorable heroes. But not everybody has the time or the patience to be polite to the bright-eyed new kid. The old guard though? The retirees and the elder heroes at the ends of their careers? Folks like Franklin Curry, the Style Champ, ACOG Ultra, and Max Damage? They were all so fantastic to me. So supportive and full of well-timed advice. Especially Max! Y'know, I still talk to Maxie every week? She's been the best mentor I could ever ask for. I just wanted to pay that kind of attention forward to the next generation and I didn't want to wait until retirement to get started."

"You just said 'not everybody has time to be polite to the bright-eyed new kid' but you're literally using your time to train several bright-eyed new kids."

"Yeah, well, I'm trying to create a culture shift of collaboration and camaraderie. I'm hoping it catches on."

"You know what else is catching on? The idea of you starring in a movie. What do you say about that, Double M?"

"I say... I already star in hundreds of movies. Every time someone records one of my deeds on a smartphone or a tablet and uploads it to the internet." She was deflecting the obvious, but she did love how many people captured her work. She'd even gone as far as filming her own response videos, adding her own commentary and thanking the fans who posted the originals.

"Haha very funny, M. But I'm being serious. You've got a legion of fans that would support an acting project."

She waved her hand at the idea. "I respect the craft far too much. I've done role-playing before. Trust me. Nobody wants to be subjected to my brand of goofy awkwardness on the big screen trying to act. I'd rather just be myself, thanks."

"A documentary then? A camera following you around giving us all a day or a week or a month in the life of Double M. I'd watch it. We all would." The host raised a hand to the masses who answered with a loud roar.

"See? That would be more my speed. But even still I couldn't do it. I'd want to give my all to a documentary and there are people in my life that wouldn't want to appear on camera." If we had watched this together, that would've been the point where Marcella gave me a squeeze. She always did that when she gave me a little low-key mention in a media appearance. The audience picked up the tone and let out a wolf whistle. To which her smile only brightened.

"People who wouldn't want to appear on camera? Sounds like forbidden love to me. Any chance you'll definitively confirm or deny the rumors about you and the Amaz—" *click*

I reached over and stopped the clip. That was enough. Darryl, to his credit, didn't even mention it. Once I took my hand off the mouse, he replaced it with his own and pulled up some tech schematics. Tech always brightened my day. I took a glance at the specifications. "What ya got there?"

He slowly took off his glasses and rubbed his eyes before responding. "I figured we needed a more stable and more secure communication system. Emails aren't instantaneous enough and standard cell phone service can be tapped into. I don't know if that'll be a problem, but I don't want to take any chances. I've been trying to design something that you and I can use continuously for this op."

"This is your communication device? What problems are you running into?" I already knew. Among other company, this would've been decent work. Next to me, though? Let's just say it was cute watching a novice make toys.

"Ummm...no problems really," he said. "It's a little bulky. But it's super secure and it fits in a pocket." He slowly turned his head in my direction and smirked.

"I see. It's point-to-point communication? Like a long-range walkie talkie? Where is that range coming from and how are you securing the transmissions?"

"I know what you're doing, y'know." He continued to smirk.

"Huh?" I played innocent.

"Huh?" he mocked. "We've worked together before, you may remember. I've been a part of this process. This thing you do where you ask questions in a way that nudges development into a new direction?"

"I'm sure I don't know what you're talking about." I unzipped my backpack and slid out my laptop.

"I'm going to send you a link that plugs you into the internal network here. In the meantime, why don't you stop fucking about and just tell me what you're thinking?" He looked over to his second monitor and opened a new email window.

I sighed. "Fine. It's big. It's big and it's handheld. If we're going to be talking back and forth on the job, I need to be able to start the conversation with a touch. I can't afford to not have both hands free. We can literally fold all this tech into a single earbud. The button mechanism can be relocated to a paper thin, biometric touchpad that can be paired with the earbud and stuck to the back of any surface. A wristband. A desk. Even a forearm. It all depends on the kind of adhesive we use. I'm sure the security features are legit. You're good at that. The security on my Supercell app has held out for all this time. But I'm honestly curious about how you plan to achieve the range you're looking for." I said all of that in a single breath while simultaneously opening the email he just sent me. I was creating my local network login when Darryl responded.

"Wow! That didn't take long! There's the girl I grew up with," he said with a laugh. "Well, as far as the broadcast range, I was thinking I could sneak a private signal onto a communication satellite, giving us exclusive access. We could also build our own simple infrastructure that only we can use. We'd have to build and place a few nodes around the country. Nothing we couldn't handle."

90

He really was brilliant. But he also really was playing catch-up. "We could do those things. Or...we could just piggyback onto a pre-existing infrastructure."

"How so?" He stopped typing. I had his attention.

"Remember the old Nextel phones? The ones with the chirp. The ones where you could use them either as phones or as walkie talkies?" Darryl nodded. "We can just tie your secure line to whatever phone service our respective phones are already using. We can even replicate the chirp sound. It's the easiest solution. Then we can just stick the digital touchpad that I mentioned right on the back of our smartphone. Assuming we don't need to put it elsewhere for tactical reasons."

"But won't the service providers notice our signal tacked onto their signal?"

"Possibly. But they wouldn't be able to decrypt it. So security isn't a concern. And I seriously doubt they'll go through much trouble to try to shut down an unobtrusive pirate signal that's being used by so few people. If we were impacting their own service, probably. If there were a couple hundred of us, undoubtedly. But at numbers this small and communication so infrequent, we'll likely go unbothered. Maybe even unnoticed. So, where are we going to fabricate this?"

"I don't have an equipped tech lab, if that's what you're asking. Is the one at your mom's still set up?"

"It is. Marce and I have been putting together our gear there for years. I'm due for a Mom visit anyway. I suppose I can just pop in once we're done redesigning your stuff here. So, let's get to it."

"Sounds good," he said. "What's with your lead though?"

I booted up my design software and cracked my knuckles. "Look, this is very sensitive operator stuff. My lead isn't someone I can just call. But they seem tapped in. If I can get them in a room, I think they can give us information about magic and the people using it."

Darryl sent me a copy of his designs before continuing. "So, who is this person and how do you know them?"

"Like I said. Operator stuff." I opened the sent files and began deconstructing them. They were kind of a mess, but I wouldn't tell Darryl that. "A few months ago, I kind of stole a contract right up from under them. The aftermath created a sort of acquaintanceship between us—though I don't know whether they'll receive me as friend or foe if I pop up asking about magic."

"Sounds like we can't let them determine the terms of engagement, then."

"No, we can't. I've got some ideas on how we can control the interaction. It'll take both of our resources. But I think we got this."

Darryl gave a quick glance my way. "You didn't answer my question earlier. Who is this person?"

"They're..." I didn't know if it was a matter of professional courtesy there. Or maybe a kind of loyalty to a person Marcella cared about. Either way, I didn't want to out them. "They're no one really. Just a random backstage crew member for stage productions. Big-budget type performances. Last I heard, they'll be traveling as part of the company for the Amazing Magisteria's upcoming US tour." It was an easy lie to tell. Close enough to the truth that any material dishonesty won't affect the plan in my head.

"Wow! Magisteria is a big deal. What's this person's name?"

"You might've seen them behind me in the power rankings. They call themself Voss13."

Chapter Nine

"It's not the first time these types of rumors have surfaced. It's really flattering if you think about it. People thinking that I'm a variant? That my magic has to be the product of superhumanity? I love it, if we're being totally honest. But I can say, unequivocally, that I do NOT have Genetic Variance Syndrome."

— *The Amazing Magisteria* on Top o' the Morning — *October 2016*

Chirp

"Ever been to Las Vegas, Darryl?" I was pacing again.

"No, of course not. Me, gamble?" The new tech was spot on. Even with just the single earbud, it sounded like he was in the room with me.

"It's not all gambling. That's sort of a common misconception. There's tons to do outside of gambling. My first time out here was actually five years ago to the day." Sigh.

"Are you serious? A twenty-first birthday trip to Las Vegas?"

"A twenty-first birthday trip to Vegas!" We laughed together at how cliché it was. "Y'see, my mother has this thing that she claims is a Jamaican tradition. When you get your first paycheck at a new job, you've got to take your family out to dinner. Much to my mother's constant annoyance, Marcella used to call her Mom 2 all the time.

"So when she hit the big leagues and signed her first contract as a professional hero in Cargill, Marcie took that tradition to heart. The signing bonus was way bigger than expected, so we skipped over dinner and went straight to the cross-country vacation." I walked over to the window and looked out for the fifth time tonight. I took yet another deep breath. I shouldn't have been that nervous.

"She swept you off your feet and took you on a whirlwind tour of Las Vegas for your twenty-first birthday with her very first big-city hero check? Wow! That sounds very much like our girl."

"We'd only just moved to our first apartment in the city, too. When we got back, we had to beg our landlord not to kick us out after the very first month of our lease because we went broke out here. We saw every show and went to every club. We partied like rockstars and tipped everyone we saw—heavily! We really showed out. And though we passed through lots of casinos, we never spent any real time in any of them."

The view from the Charlemagne suite of the Paris Hotel & Casino was breathtaking. You could see the whole strip from up here. Most people enjoy it for the close-up vantage of the hotel's signature half-size replica of the Eiffel Tower, but I was looking past all that and taking in the sight of Bellagio's water fountains.

The bright lights were almost blinding but that's not why I had to wipe away a tear. When Marcella brought me out here that first time, that's where we stayed. She knew how much I'd love the water fountains. I still did.

"It sounds like a lot of fun was had. Did you two ever come back after that?"

"Not together," I said. "She's had conventions out here and I've taken some local contracts. But once I started my career as an operator, being seen with me became a detriment to her career. This place is made of cameras." I didn't mean for that to be another dig at Darryl and how my operating career got started. But I didn't mind if he took it as one either.

"Where did you take her? When you got your first operator check?" Darryl asked. He might've been trying to move past the unpleasantness. I'd allow it.

"There's a place up in Toronto. I don't even know if it's still open. But we signed up for a sort of science fiction fantasy camp. You join a class of about a half-dozen people and they let you experience elements from your favorite movies. There were space-flight simulators, blaster gun combat arenas, and laser sword training. All of it complete with well-produced sets, realistic replicas, and costumes.

"It was a weekend of doing action movie stuff, safely for once, and of correcting the organizers about the nature of the tech they were simulating." I could still picture Marcella's face after she knocked down a condescending trainer and lectured him at the point of a laser sword. It was the most fun I'd ever seen her have.

But that was us all over. She used her first check to bring me somewhere that suited her personality, Vegas, that still allowed me to be in the thick of things while engaging almost exclusively with her.

Then I used my first check to take her somewhere far more subdued, with far fewer people, that still helped her make reality out of make-believe.

Until now, I had never really considered how much those trips mirrored our youth together. With the lab in my mom's basement, I gave her a space to turn her creative sketches into real tech. Then, to create our best work together, she facilitated my need to have a fun group of people to be around and care about.

"I'm sure she loved that. A weekend of living in the future? It sounds pretty amazing." Suddenly, I remembered who exactly funded that trip.

"Yeah. It was. I suppose I have you to thank for that." It was a little unsteadying to acknowledge how much overlap our lives have had even during the years when we were apart. I didn't want to dwell much deeper into that thought while we were still on the job. "Time check?"

"The window of opportunity that we've designated opens in about 30 minutes and lasts for another 30 after that. Lots of time to ease back and focus. Do you need me to stay on the line until then?"

"No, I'm gonna go over the layout up here again. You can never be too prepared. I'll call you when it's done."

"Okay. Let me know how it goes. Happy birthday, Sana."
Chirp

Do you know how long it takes to track down and capture an elite operator? Apparently, it takes several months. Darryl knew that, because he and Mark had been planning for almost a year before drawing me to that campaign fundraiser in Hewlett, North Carolina and then basically inviting me to the rec center in Ohio. He used mission notes from every contract I'd ever filled for him to create a profile of everything I was likely to know going into a job. Then he crafted a job that could still effectively leave me in the dark while not giving off any glaring red flags. As paranoid as I usually am? It wasn't easy. I was beginning to understand the process, because it was taking forever to capture Voss13.

It'd taken so long to set up this mission that I've fallen in the power rankings. To keep my activities a complete secret, Darryl couldn't put me under a contract for any of what we were planning for Phase Two, in case our targets also had access to the operator database. A legitimate operations contract would have my approximate mission locations and my estimated time of completion. Concessions are made in the rankings to accommodate for operators on long drawn out missions. But the lack of a contract meant that my operations profile would have gone dormant. Marking the slow and steady decline of a status I put a lot of effort into building. In my absence, it was high profile jobs, like the fake one we'd set up, that put Voss in the top spot.

The premise was simple: Contract Voss for a job and be there when they arrived. The difficulty was in figuring out where they might be, what job they might accept, and how to merge the two. That last bit was the real clincher. I was using both their celebrity presence and my personal experience with them as the basis for my plan.

I guessed that they only liked taking jobs within cities where they were already scheduled to appear. The night we met on the job, the Amazing Magisteria had a book signing on the other side of town. There were a handful of other disappearances along their itinerary as well. I assumed that this was a matter of energy expenditure. Maybe the closer they were to a target, the less power they'd have to use getting in and getting out. That was as close to a working theory as we had.

As a client, Darryl would be able to post a contract to the job boards and set terms that appeared favorable to attract our quarry. Difficult parameters, high pay, complete disappearance required. That would weed out most potential applicants. Then we'd need to arrange an environment we could control. It would have to appear as a trap for a target, when it was really a trap for Voss.

City after city of their latest tour went by and we were unable to strike. The conditions needed to be near perfect. Either we couldn't secure a workable location, or we couldn't secure it in time to issue the contract early enough, and even once all the pieces fell into place, we'd only get one chance at this. If multiple similar-sounding contracts from the same client began appearing on the wire at every stop on Magisteria's tour, they'd get suspicious. Voss13 would go to ground. Everything had to be precise without looking that way.

Though we scouted several earlier cities, the logistical stars didn't start to align until we began scouting Las Vegas. Once that became apparent, I reserved the suite, Darryl posted the contract, and

Voss soon accepted it. The Amazing Magisteria had a huge televised performance at the MGM Grand — the crown jewel of the tour was happening barely half a mile away from the hotel we set for the operation. We had reserved the best available penthouse we could find, because we knew we wouldn't be disturbed. It ended up being at the Paris. From the outside, no one would be able to see what was happening in the room. Even still, we set up the trap in a central area to minimize how much sound might escape. Not that it would matter. In a city like Las Vegas, the sound of a lot of physical activity coming from a hotel room is standard. We really couldn't have picked a more perfect location. To Voss, the hotel would appear as an ideal place to catch a target with lots of entrances or exits. We'd already gotten eyes on all of them, including the door we planned our prey to walk in through. After taking what seemed like my hundredth walkthrough, I sat down on the bed with my head in my hands. I still had a little more than ten minutes to spare when it happened.

Familiar music started playing. I started mouthing the words before I even registered the source. It was my phone. This is what happens when you space out reminiscing about happier times. All this preparation and I forgot to put my phone on silent. It's simple things like this that ruin ops. This wasn't even Darryl hitting me on the secure digital chirp line either. That would at least be tactical support. This was "Cosmic Girl" by Jamiroquai. Marcella's personal ringtone. I didn't want to answer while I was on the job. But I should've told myself that before I hit the green answer button. So much for professionalism.

"Hey!"

"Hey!" She paused. "Sana, I know we're not... I know we're not together. But I still love you. So, I wanted to wish you a happy birthday. I didn't want you to think I'd forgotten."

Amazing how stressful this felt. Especially just after a relatively chill conversation with Darryl.

"I love you too. This means a lot to me. It's been a really hard few months for me and knowing that you still care makes it all a bit easier."

"I'm always gonna care, even if what we were doing before was unsustainable. You're still you and I'm still me. I'm always gonna care about you."

"Thanks, Marce. Thanks for reaching out. Thanks for being so patient with me."

"I want to see you, Sana. Can I see you?"

"I don't know if that would be a good idea. My schedule isn't easy to nail down right now and I'm on the road a lot."

She laughed her warm laugh; the real one you don't see on TV. "I meant now, silly. Can we video chat? I figure since you've got the time to talk, maybe we can look at each other while we do. This is the longest we've ever gone without seeing each other."

She was right. The last time we'd been apart for more than a few weeks had been that goodwill tour she'd done in Europe and Asia, and even then, we'd video chatted several times a week. I'd missed her laughter so much. But I saw her face all the time, even now. It was impossible to avoid any time I turned on a TV or scrolled through any social media feed or walked outside at all. "That's definitely not a good idea."

"Why not?"

I frowned. I could hear her frustration. "My location is...mission sensitive right now. I can't tell you or even give you an indication of where I am. I'm sorry. I really wish I could."

"Oh. Well, I noticed that you fell a few spots in the rankings. I know how much those mean to you. Are you okay? Is this because of the big job you're on?" Was she fishing for information or trying to keep me on the line because she missed me like I missed her? I thought it was the latter, but I also thought we'd be together all our lives.

"I'm okay. It'll be fine. I mean...I hate dropping in the ranks. But it's not the most important thing right now. If I could get into the details, I would. You know how it is."

She sighed loudly. "I do know how it is. I'm still me...and you're still you. Goodbye, Sana. Stay safe out there."

She hung up before I could respond. It was like disappointing her was all I knew how to do anymore, and it was getting to me. I didn't even have time to process everything I was feeling because I had to get into character. Voss would be here soon and there needed to be a cold, hard bitch here waiting for them.

I turned off my phone and got to work.

I took one last look out the bedroom window before drawing the curtains completely. The entire suite was dark and silent. The only exception was the bathroom, where I left on the faucet and a single light. I cracked the door before waiting in my designated spot. Whether entering by door or portal, Voss would immediately spot the illumination, hear the sounds, and focus their attention towards a target that wasn't there. They'd cross the living room, enter the bedroom, and then turn left towards the bathroom. But I'd be waiting to the right. I got into position, leaning up against the wall that connected the bedroom and the living room.

My armor had light-manipulating tech. When faced with fast moving kinetic energy, like a melee attack or a projectile weapon, it hardened as a shield and glanced off the incoming threat. Times like now, when I was perfectly still, it shifted the light, rendering me near invisible. Even without wearing a mask to help me blend into the darkness, I'd be almost impossible to spot until I started moving. This functionality was inspired by Marcella and I having watched too many movies. That's why we called it Predator mode. Only my armor had it though. Stealth was not a part of Double M's repertoire.

I needed to stop thinking about her.

When the designated time hit, I tensed for action, knowing Voss would be as ready to strike as I was. Only a few minutes passed before I felt the faint rustle of air displacement. A light without a source appeared into the middle of the living room area then expanded to the size of a person. Voss had created a portal just like the one they were making when I first saw them. Once they stepped through, the portal disappeared with a soft but audible pop.

They didn't even scan in my direction to clear the room. Why would they? A bathroom trip was completely plausible for anyone. As soon as I saw them, I was in motion. From my position, I only had to reach out. Stun baton in hand, I didn't even need to fully extend my arm. Voss was down at least two seconds before they would've seen me. I paused over the body and wondered if I could integrate the stun tech into my armor. Later. For now, I grabbed some rope out of my kit.

When Voss woke up, a few minutes later, they were bound and gagged. Their eyes widened in recognition and they began to shout into the ball wedged in their mouth. I put up a calming hand and slowly removed the gag. "What the fuck is this about, JC? If you wanted another tumble, you could've just asked. You know I'm good for it."

"Look, I'm sorry about this, Voss. I need some information and you're gonna give it to me. Please don't make me hurt you."

"You're not gonna hurt me! I'm a bloody friend of the family, ain't I? Now, let me out of this rope!" They were half-right. I didn't want to hurt them, but I absolutely would. The stakes were too high.

"I'm looking for any information you can give me about certain magic users."

"And what? Because I use magic, I'm supposed to know who you're looking for? Do you think we all know each other? All hang out on the weekends? Do you have any idea how bigoted you sound right now? I don't come to your place of employment and ask if you know all the other black operators, do I?" Voss was trying to rile me up, force a mistake, but I wasn't number one—well, hadn't been number one—for nothing. They needed to know I wasn't fucking around, so I pulled out their wand. I made to break it between my thumbs and forefingers. "Easy, girl! Easy! Don't do that. That's my livelihood. That's *both* of my livelihoods. I was only joking. I know who you're looking for. Untie me and we can talk."

"Oh, *now* you know them?" I laughed. "That seems a little too easy. I haven't even given you any details yet."

They smirked at me. "Oh you haven't? As if you've even got any details to give, you fucking arsehole. If you had any details, you wouldn't be fucking about with me." They started laughing. "JC, you're an American and looking for mages. There aren't many of us active in America and, outside of schools, none of us are really all that pally with one another. So, if you're looking for 'certain magic-users'— 'users' *plural*—there's not a lot to choose from, is there? Plus, you've fallen six spaces in the power rankings in just a few months. Either you're off your game, and that's not bloody likely given our current situation, or you're on some long, complicated mission that'll get you back on top. There's only one set of American mages that's even worth the hassle."

I was stunned. I knew Voss would be a valuable lead, but I wasn't expecting all of this. If this was how they always operated, they damn sure earned that top spot. I'd never tell *them* that though.

Instead, I pretended to not be impressed at all. "Start talking, then. Maybe we can wrap this up early."

"Interested in the narrative now, are we?" Voss cocked their head, assessing me. I had no idea what they saw. "Look, on principle, I'm not telling you nothing while you've got me tied up like this."

"And if I let you out, you'll tell me what I want to know? Because if I untie you and you start fighting me, it's not gonna go well for you."

"It'd go better than you think," Voss said with a smile, the tattoos on their skin beginning to glow faintly, then fade out. "But no. Here's how this goes: you're going to untie me and give me back my wand and let me leave here to do my show. You'll meet me backstage afterwards. Then and only then will I tell you what you want to know."

I decided for one last bluff. "That's an awful lot of terms you're setting from such a weak position, Voss. You might've noticed that I already have you here at my mercy."

Voss gave me a look that I'm pretty sure they stole that from Double M. "I said I'm a friend of the family, you smug cunt. Your girl wouldn't like you doing this, would she? Had you just asked, we'd be having a laugh right now and talking about the ones you're after. I'm no friend to them. But seeing as how you had no reason to know that, I'm willing to mostly overlook this bit of unpleasantness. But now you owe me. So, do what I said and let's end this evening on a pleasant note."

I didn't know them well enough to be sure they were sincere, but nothing was pinging my radar. I guess, worst case scenario, I could just skip to big and loud Plan B: sneak into their next tour date and stun them again in their dressing room.

"Alright, Voss. We'll play it your way." Whipping out my long knife, I cut them free and handed back the wand. They looked relieved to have it back, in perhaps the only real moment of vulnerability they'd shown me yet.

"Good choice." They took a moment to regain their composure. "All right, I'll leave you a VIP ticket with backstage access at will-call. After each show, the crew and I have some fun times with the fans. You'll be with me for that. Then we can talk. Fair?"

"Leave the tickets under the name 'Jace Clementine.' You're not gonna make me regret this are you, Voss?"

With a wink, they said, "Oh, you'll get what you came for, Jace." Unbound, they quickly regained their swagger. I wasn't used to being referred to by my fake first name, and it sat wrong with me, especially with Voss.

As I went back to the restroom to splash my face, I could hear them conjure another portal to leave by. All I could do was place my head in my hands and hope I wasn't making a mistake. I could make a status check with Darryl but what would I say? "Sorry, I had our mark at my mercy, but I let them go. Now I'm heading to a magic show and a backstage party." That wouldn't fly. It was on-the-job improvisation and Darryl wouldn't understand. He wasn't expecting a call yet anyway. Sure, he'd notice when several hours passed and he hadn't heard back. But if this all paid off, it won't matter how long this part took. This was my job and my decision.

Chapter Ten

"I wasn't trying to start an industry. I was trying to get out of sex work. Period. I loved it and made a great living on my back. But I knew I didn't want to do it forever. So, being a Vegas girl, I played the odds. I found a perfect hand, weighed the risk, and bet big. It all felt too good to be true, so when the ride looked like it was over and I was eventually caught, I didn't fight it. When the cops showed up asking about the murder, I didn't even deny it. When they ultimately released me from prison, I never tried to be an operator under the new laws. I retreated and lived a quiet life. I won big once and I didn't want to take a chance at losing it all."

— For Hire Special Edition Issue *on Alice Proctor, the first operator*

Walking to and walking through the MGM Grand was difficult, this night of all nights. Everything reminded me of an experience from five years ago today. The latest assaults to my memory were these exact sights and sounds as Marcella and I made our way to the KÀ Theater to take in a lavish production of acrobatics and martial arts. It was one of the most amazing things I'd ever seen.

The show I was heading to was in the Garden Arena, a different stage in the same complex. Moving towards the box office, I couldn't help but take notice of the people. The casino floor between me and my destination was packed. This time of night on the Las Vegas Strip is perpetually packed, but this was Saturday night in the moments before a performance by the Amazing Magisteria. Between the chatter of the crowds and the cacophony of the gaming machines, it was surprising that I could even hear my own thoughts.

I arrived at the box office about twenty minutes before the show began. There was a long line ahead of me, but I wasn't worried about arriving late. True to Voss's word, there was a ticket waiting at will-call listed under my alias. I caught a bit of a weird vibe from the ticket agent when she noticed what seat I had reserved. She looked at her computer screen and then gave me a bit of a smirk. When I took a look at the tickets themselves, I saw that I had a second-row seat right next to what was normally an orchestra pit. I couldn't place whether the agent's reaction was based on the relative expense of the tickets or something else. Either way, I had no time to really process anything except my next move, which was to go find my seat.

The show's announcers were issuing a few final statements over the loudspeakers as I walked in. Advertisements from the hotel announcing other available shows and features. Warnings about all the strobing lights and loud noises that the performance would employ. I took in all this information and more as the ushers pointed me from section to section. The lights began to dim as I was finally led to my row. I was able to shimmy past several other attendees and plop down into my chair just as playing cards began to rain from ceiling.

"Catch one!" called a booming voice with an Australian accent. "Catch one! And if you can't catch one, pick one up off the ground. And if you can't do that, have someone pass you a card. Everybody should be holding one." The low throng of ambient music started to play. Ethereal strings building atmosphere as we each gathered a card. I held mine up to the faint light to see that I secured a queen of diamonds. "Examine the card you've got. Show them to your neighbor. Hell, trade them with your neighbor, if you like. Just make sure you're holding a single card by the end. Of. This. Sentence."

With that, a spotlight shone from behind the audience to the center of the stage. The curtains began to draw back. In front of a cerulean blue backdrop, a small but sharply pronounced silhouette appeared. As the shadow began to move, I could start to make out the details. Clad in a traditional tuxedo, white gloves, a black bow tie, and high heels, the Amazing Magisteria took the stage. They were making some rapid hand motions that I couldn't quite make out due to the lighting.

It seemed a bit strange that while Magisteria was towards the back of the stage, the spotlight hadn't moved from the very center. Rather than the light moving to meet the performer, the performer was striding confidently forward to meet the light. As they got closer, I could finally see that the steadily quickening hand motions were to accommodate the shuffling of more playing cards. Their fingers were a blur as they appeared to hold a deck of cards in each hand. They were alternating between shuffling one, then the other, then both at the same time—all while cycling through several different shuffling methods. It was stunning. Their feet never stopped moving either. They walked all the way up to the center of the spotlight and that's when the magic started.

Instead of walking into and then out of the beam, the Amazing Magisteria started to ascend upwards as if the illumination of the spotlight were a ramp to the heavens. The music shifted from ethereal strings to thrashing metal ones as they gathered all the cards in their hands and started throwing them into the crowd one by one. First in high-arching overhands and then in casual flicks of the wrist. More and more playing cards shot from Magisteria's hands as they strode back and forth, up and down along the luminescence of the spotlight. "Catch one!" they called to the crowd again.

While all our eyes were glued to the impossible scene above us, the stage had filled with the show's other cast members. A team of dancers wore stripped down versions of Magisteria's own tuxedo and performed a choreographed routine. A series of swings, trapezes, and trampolines had been erected on stage for a high-flying acrobatics exhibition. Both would've been truly impressive...if there wasn't a person literally floating through the sky right above our heads. The acrobats, at least, served a dual function. At the heights of their jumps and somersaults, the aerialists were tossing objects over to Magisteria as they continued to dance through the air on an unbroken beam of light.

The objects were hard to identify in mid-air. It was only after Magisteria caught them did they make sense as fresh decks of cards to replace the ones they had already tossed into the audience. Each new deck was similarly given away with individual flair. One deck was pinched at the top and bottom forcing all fifty-two cards to spray and a long stream. "Catch one!" they called out again. The next deck was held in their left hand and fanned out, gunslinger-style, to the crowd with their right. "Catch one!" Yet another was flung in a three-hundred- and sixty-degrees arc as Magisteria twirled in an amazingly fast pirouette.

After several decks of cards had made their way into the crowd, Magisteria descended the beam, right down to the center of the spotlight on stage, just as the dancers and acrobats were finishing their routines. They all completed their performances right as the show's main event set their first foot back on the ground, did a graceful spin to face their raucous fans, and took a bow. The rest of the cast waited a beat before taking a bow of their own, then they quickly moved off stage leaving their leader by themself.

"Welcome! Welcome everybody to my twentieth anniversary show! I've been doing this a long time and it's always a bit of hassle coming up with new ways to dazzle my discerning fans." Only Voss could sound charming while essentially expressing frustration with the people that made them famous. "This is all very tiring. Do you mind if I have a seat?" It was impossible to gauge a real answer from the audience. They hadn't stopped screaming since their favorite performer appeared. Magisteria took the continued noise as an affirmative and whipped out their wand from an inside pocket. With an elaborate hand gesture, they conjured what could only be described as a cloud of smoke and fire. First, they hopped onto the cloud. Then, they crouched down into a sitting position as the cloud rose a few feet into the air, giving them a perch to look over the crowd with. They looked utterly relaxed. After defying gravity for several minutes, they now looked like they were on a couch at a party, addressing a few friends.

"Did you catch one of the cards I threw? Did you? Let's see them then! If you've got two cards...one of the ones that rained from the ceiling and one of the ones I threw out, hold them up." The backdrop at the far edge of the stage was revealed to be a massive video monitor. As people began holding up their two cards, that monitor acted as a livestream for the camera crews moving down the aisles of the theater. Each audience member that the cameras approached was holding two identical cards. Even the man in the seat next to mine was holding a twin pair of four of clubs. He nearly lost his mind when the cameras got to him and he showed them the matched set. I had reached for that second card myself. A group of them had flown from Magisteria's hands right down to our section. I zeroed in on one and right before I could reach for it, the much taller gentleman next to me snatched it. I wondered if his second four of clubs would right now be a second queen of diamonds, if I held it.

"So, wait! You caught two separate cards from two different sources? And they match? How is that possible? Oh my! It must be magic!" They laughed at their own joke. It didn't matter how silly they

113

were, though. The audience ate it up. I did too. They were incredible, and the rest of the performance was fantastic as well. Even better than all the ones Marcella made me watch on television. Despite knowing that the magic was real and that Magisteria was never in any danger, I finally got a bit into the thrill of the thing. Marcella would be proud.

Once the stage show was over, I let the crowd around me slowly filter out before I made my way backstage. It took a long while as the audience was thick and most were in a hurry to use the access they had to get to meet their hero. By the time I used my VIP pass to get through to the backstage area, the party there was already jumping. I walked slowly along the outside of the room, taking it all in from the relative safety of having the wall at my back. The music was loud, and the place was packed with fans fawning over members of the crew, the other performers, and Magisteria themself.

They were still amazing to watch, but this time for a different reason. There was a certain level of care that they had for their fans. For the younger ones, Magisteria got down on a knee or threw an arm over a shoulder. I couldn't hear what was being said but I could tell that the words were far more meaningful than the autographs those kids were getting. Their faces lit up when Magisteria spoke to them. They launched into huge hugs and were warmly received. Sometimes it's okay to meet your heroes.

For the older fans, Magisteria took lots of photos. I still couldn't hear the words above the din of the crowd, but the body language always read as that of old friends seeing each other after an extended absence. It was incredible to watch. This was still the same smug asshole who had a successful side-hustle vanishing people to the bottom of the sea. The same hired assassin who I only met after stealing one of their kills. Yet here, they made everybody feel like a valued member of the family. The level of comfort everyone had was striking. None of it read as inauthentic either.

This was the first time I'd met another operator with a day job, and they made it seem effortless. If they could make both identities as Voss13 and Amazing Magisteria work...why couldn't I? Why did everything feel so much more complicated for me?

Was I doing it to myself?

After a certain hour, the younger fans were escorted out along with the parents and guardians. The remaining adults, mainly the crew and some VIPs, began grouping up, growing more familiar with their touches. I wondered if this was my cue to move on. When I looked around for Magisteria, they were in street clothes, Voss again, their cocky little smile fixed on me, holding the rope and the gag that I thought I had left in the hotel room.

I hid my nerves behind a grin and moved toward them.

Chapter Eleven

"When I was a kid in Australia, I saw a magician from America on TV. He was just a guest on a late-night talk show. Not too unlike your own. I don't even remember his name. It doesn't matter. What mattered is that I saw him and I immediately knew what I wanted to do. I watched and went to every magic show I could. I started practicing on the school yard. Doing card tricks in my bedroom. Creating my own illusions in mall parking lots. It only took thousands of hours of hard work and BOOM! Now I'm the Amazing Magisteria and, if you work had enough, you could be too!"

— *The Amazing Magisteria on* The Shae Livingston Show

We went through a set of double doors to a small, cramped access hallway. Voss didn't even glance in either direction before creating a new portal. "Come on then, Jace." They held out their hand.

I reached out and they threaded their long, pale fingers through mine. I looked down at our hands as I stepped through, using them as an anchor point to block out the strangeness of traveling through an actual portal. My mind tried to pin down the science of it all but couldn't.

I stepped into the spacious living room of a fancy apartment or house. An entire wall was made of windows; outside, I saw the ocean.

Which ocean, I had no idea. The room was stark, white, and mostly bare. It was devoid of character in a way that startled me. It looked like a model from a television show about very, very rich people. Then I turned to look behind me and saw framed photographs, dozens of them, with people I recognized and didn't. Some were in color, some black and white. The purple of Marcella's hair caught my eye. It was a selfie, her and Voss, and they were both grinning ear to ear. Voss was in street clothes and they were both disheveled. I knew that glow, Marce's glow of happiness when she had real feelings for someone. I'd been looking at that glow for years, but I couldn't remember the last time I'd seen it.

For the first time since high school, I felt a stab of jealousy.

It wasn't that Marcella didn't love anyone else. All she knew how to do was love. But in all our time together, I'd heard about crushes, sat with her through heartbreak, adored her fangirling, and of course occasionally watched others give her pleasure. But the depth of her feelings for Voss...I'd missed them completely, even though they'd probably been all over her face.

I was jealous because I didn't know if I'd see that look again for me.

"Jace? You all right, girl?" Voss's voice had softened. I turned around and really looked at them, beyond the hard edges of the operator Voss13 and the gregariousness of The Amazing Magisteria. I tried to see everything Marcella saw.

But how could I? I didn't know this person the way she did.

117

"You know what I see when I look at you, JC?" Voss asked in that lower voice. "I see that you're tired."

I looked at them and I saw it too.

"Yeah," they said. "Me too, sometimes. It's the life, isn't it? Can't even talk to her about it." They motioned to the photo. Then they touched under a ridge and a panel slid to reveal a bar. "You want a drink?"

I shook my head.

"Suit yourself." They poured themself whisky. Expensive whisky. "I thought we'd come here, play a bit, and talk shop. But I've got the feeling you need a little something more right now." They sat down on the pristine white couch in the middle of the room. "Sit with me?"

They set their drink down on the glass coffee table and we faced each other. I brushed their hair back the way I had that first night, and they smiled at me—a cocky smile, but a fond one. Those long fingers came up to touch my face, and I closed my eyes, savoring the sensation as they trailed a path down my neck to my collarbone.

Then we were kissing, and there was heat to it, but comfort as well. We made out like teenagers on that couch, until I was physically aching for them.

"Do you trust me?" they asked.

"No," I said.

"Will you try?" They held up the rope, and I offered my wrists. They winked at me and leaned in.

They'd been wrong. We did play, but it wasn't the kind of play either of us had been expecting. It was…joyful, connective, but all the while so very, very hot. I'd spent so much time over the years with sex being a release, another adrenaline rush, that I'd forgotten what it was like to have a first time with someone that was deeper. We already knew a little bit about each other, and from there we increased our knowledge. It was hours of touching, of teasing, of demanding more from our bodies than they wanted to give. In the living room, we had found each other's sensitive spots. In the bedroom, we'd tested each other's limits on smooth sheets that soothed heated skin.

Then, after a particularly blinding orgasm, my stomach growled, and we burst into laughter.

"Chinese?" they asked, and I nodded eagerly.

That was how we found ourselves eating noodles in bed, me on my side so my ass didn't encounter anything that would increase the sting.

Voss was back to teasing me—the verbal, infuriating kind. "Easier to eat if you sit up."

"Go fuck yourself," I said cheerfully, inhaling the lo mein.

"Gotta regain your strength, I suppose." They waggled their eyebrows at me.

I gave them the finger around my chopsticks.

We ate in companionable silence for a bit.

"M mentioned that you two started as a team. Why'd you quit the superhero game?" They stuck their chopsticks back in the carton

119

and placed both on a bedside table. "If what's fueling you is the same what's fueling our girl, you'd have been awesome at it."

I smiled a bit at her being referred to as *our girl*, even though I knew that wasn't really the case anymore. I had no idea if Voss knew as well. That wasn't the part of their statement that I wanted to get into. "What's fueling me?" I said.

They laughed. "Don't worry. Your secret's safe. She never told me the details. She says you've been together since high school, back before you had powers. So I assume you've got the same origin story."

"Yeah. Yeah, we do." I got the impression that they would accept any honest answer regardless of how vague, being an operator themself. Came with the territory. "I suppose it ties into that origin story. After what happened...happened, Marce wanted to connect with the world and I just wanted to retreat from it."

"Connecting with the world is what she does best." We exchanged a grin.

"You're not wrong and you can probably tell that I'm a bit more guarded than that. Superhero work requires a personal touch that I just can't generate. Of course, I could've kept going through the motions. I gave it my best. It just never would've been a satisfying life for me."

"Fair enough. Just going through the motions, though, you still might have made it onto the rankings. With talent like yours, maybe even all the way to number one?"

I appreciated the compliment from someone as competitive as Voss, although I didn't agree with their assessment. *For Hire* allowed

120

superhumans registered as a group onto the rankings together. As a duo, Double M could've dragged any partner all the way up the charts. Me, as a solo superhero though? "No. Probably not. I'm just better suited as a top-tier operator."

They nodded and reached for their carton of noodles. "By the by, I had a contract. I better get paid and get a five-star rating for the things I'm about to tell you. I'm not losing my new top spot because of this."

I let myself feel the twinge over that until it was gone.

"I'll make sure that happens."

"Appreciated." They were back in operator mode. "So you were asking about magic users."

"And you said you knew them." I felt myself tense up. What if it had all been a trick?

"I do. They call themselves The Imperative, the arrogant fucks." So says a person who publicly calls themself The Amazing Magisteria. "It's three of them, two gals and a bloke. All really powerful. They've been controlling your government for a couple of decades. It was a sort of game they played. A little push here, a little nudge there, a memory wipe or two, and they pretty much run the whole show."

"Why? What's their motivation?"

"Boredom?" They saw the look on my face. "You'd be surprised. You do this long enough, power's the only thing that's interesting anymore. There aren't too many of us, mages, as I said. None of us want the word to get out about us. No one wants to share the wealth. We're not like the variants; the normals wouldn't leave us alone if they knew we could bend reality. So we mostly lay low or make our own lives plush. A few of us, though, want to make the most of our powers. There aren't any more slots left for world famous magicians. I've already got that sewn up. These three decided to take over your country. Didn't take them too long either. Once they had it in hand though, it stopped being a game and started up as an obsession. They ain't giving it back easy." They paused for a mouthful of Singapore noodles, but it felt like a dramatic pause nonetheless. Voss, Magisteria—whichever the name, they were enjoying the audience.

"Why do you know this much about them? You said you're not that pally with other...mages."

"They're powerful, The Imperative is. Almost as powerful as I am, really. So, they asked me to join up, back before I made my big splash. I couldn't think of anything more boring than dabbling in your freakshow American politics. Plus, mages overextend themselves and die all the time. I didn't want to take a chance at burning out just to learn a whole new discipline of magic. So, I politely declined. I even stayed friendly with the one, Circe, for a bit. That was before they decided that my celebrity was a threat to their secrecy. They tried to have a go at me, it all went poorly for them, and now I'm telling you their secrets. So, I guess they got it right, after all." They cackled.

Circe. A name from Greek mythology, but that's all I could remember. "I don't suppose there are any tips you could give me to take them down."

122

"I can do better." They grabbed the phone from the back pocket of their jeans, which were lying on the floor. As they leaned down, I thought about grabbing their ass, but I decided against it. Didn't want to be distracted and, honestly, my body could use the break. They flipped through their photos. "The thing with magic is that it takes a feed, a focus, and time to charge. The bigger or more complicated the spell, the longer you gotta charge it before activating. Oh, this one here is Circe." They turned their screen in my direction and showed me a picture of a large older woman with dark hair. She had her arms around Voss in a big bear hug. I could only see her face in profile. Both were smiling, though nowhere near as giddy as the picture of Voss and Marcella.

"Better times?"

"Something like that. We had a sweet thing going. Then we didn't. Her and her friends tried to murder me. It happens." Their nonchalance read as forced, but it wasn't my place to pry. I'd be keeping Voss out of this as a thank you for the information. "Anyway...the feed is our source. The powers we've studied. The masters we've each learned from. It's not an inherent thing. We've had to earn our abilities, and each is etched into our skin." They began flipping through the photos on their phone again as I began to study the arcane tattoos all over their body. Of course, I'd seen them before...but I hadn't really looked before now. The woman in the picture, Circe, had them as well.

"Is there a way to cut off that source?"

"No... it's always inside of us. It's what keeps some of us young. You can separate them from their focus though. The object we choose to channel our power through."

"Like your wand?"

"And Circe's baton, Hale's staff, and Araña's chains. Won't be easy though. The first thing any of us learn are low-cost protection spells to keep our objects safe. Plus, Araña keeps her chains bound to her wrist and ankles at all times. Here's her."

I was still considering the idea of someone choosing to remain chained forever when I looked at Voss' phone again. The dark-haired woman looking back at me...was adorable. Her look was charming and sweet, her tattoos were colorful and vibrant—not at all like the dark marks covering Voss or Circe's bodies. "Mental, that one. Completely unhinged. Don't let the cute face fool you. Whereas Circe is in it for the power trip, and Hale's a zealot who believes in some bullshit divine right to rule, Araña is just a sadist. She likes control. She likes to hurt. Not like our fun from before, either. Her skill is prodigious, but she'll just as soon choke the life out of you with those chains." It was tough picturing such an angelic beauty as the type of person Voss described, but I suppose looks were deceiving.

"What do you mean 'her skill is prodigious'?"

They paused for a moment to come up with an analogy I'd understand. "You're American. Think guns. If I have a small gun, I can shoot you. Bang. Longer barrel, longer shot, bigger boom, right? Imagine if you had a gun with a barrel like an infinity symbol. The bullet would just loop 'round and 'round picking up speed until you opened one end and aimed it at your unfortunate target. Obviously, physics doesn't allow for that. Magic does. Araña can create an infinite loop with her chains that strengthens everything she does. It technically makes her more powerful than mages with a larger feed to draw from because it doesn't take her as long to charge even master level spells."

"If I was going to guess, I'd say she should be my first target."

"What? Because she's their powerhouse? No... I'm not telling you how to do your job, but I'd shut down Hale first. Take out a strategist and still leave the other two feeling overconfident about the remaining odds." They gave me the phone one last time for me to see a heavily muscular man with a tattooed sleeve on each arm. In the picture, he was shirtless and standing over an equally shirtless Voss. They caught the look on my face as I took in the situation in front of me. "Just because I don't really like that religious jackass, didn't mean I couldn't roll around with him a bit. This was years ago, though. Circe actually took this picture...before she tried to kill me."

"Same day? Like right after the sex?" I grinned. "I could see it."

"Your girl was right. You're kinda funny when you aren't being so serious."

It was one thing to think about Marcella in regard to her relationship with Voss. That was good. It made me happy, even, to think these two people brought happiness to each other. But it was another thing to realize that I was doing operator work, work I couldn't share with her, with her partner. Who also couldn't tell her.

125

"Oh, quit it with the long face. You two love each other. You'll figure it out." Voss took my hand. They did know about our break. "Easier if it's lower stakes, like she and I. We get the high points, the fun times, sure. But you get to wake up with her, go to sleep with her. You have holidays together. A life built together. It's something, JC. It's a nice something."

I wondered when the last time was that they'd had that something themself.

"But we're not here to discuss that," they reminded me.

I sat up, pushing the thought of Marcella aside. "So... how do I kill The Imperative? Can I just shoot them?"

"Americans and their guns, yeah? Well, finding them will be the harder part, but yeah...I suppose you can just shoot them. They'd have to be taken by surprise or separated from their focus objects before they could react. I don't know what your abilities really are, but I doubt you could stand and trade with any of them in a straight fight." Their tattoos began to glow. The lights in the room flickered. "Once they're lit up, your time is beyond up."

I put the now-empty carton of noodles on the bedside table. "What else?"

Voss picked theirs back up. "I've got nothing. No location, no care to know. They stay in their corner, I stay in mine."

"I may have to kill them."

Voss shrugged, and though I'd seen real pain in their eyes when they brought up Circe, I did not see regret. "Can't say I'd feel one way or another at this point."

I believed them. "Sorry about tying you up and everything, earlier." I put my clothes on.

"Well, I wasn't sorry to return the favor." They glowed again, and a portal opened. Through it, I could see the Bellagio fountains in the near distance. "The real name's Charlie, by the way."

"Sana."

"Good luck to you, Sana. You'll need it."

Chapter Twelve

"The cops been busting our heads long before the day I became the so-called Hero of Glenville. Yeah, I disarmed everybody fighting but it wasn't some play at equal sides. If I didn't disarm those cops, they'd have shot down my friends and neighbors. If I didn't disarm those nation brothers, they'd have killed some of those cops. That would've flooded the hood with a thousand more cops. The block would've been hotter than ever. When the city offered me a job, I thought they were asking me to do the same oppressive bullshit they were doing. I said 'Hell nah! I'll be a cop when you stop letting those racist white cops out on our streets.' I flipped the mayor's desk over and stormed on outta there. They came knocking on my door the very next morning and told me I had a deal."

— For Hire Special Edition Issue *on Franklin Curry, the first superhero*

"What did you end up buying?" I was back in Ronnie's shitty SUV. In the front seat this time.

"I'm sorry, ma'am?" Ma'am? He was trying to stay on his best behavior with me. It was cute.

"Last time I saw you, Frost said he was giving you a bonus to spend on yourself. I expected to be picked up in a hovercar this time. No such luck." I don't know why I enjoyed needling this kid, but I did.

"My sister had been engaged for about three years. Her and her fiancé weren't able to set a date. They couldn't afford a wedding, so I paid for it." Ugh! Levity aborted. This kid was just too sweet to properly hate.

The rest of the trip was silent. I didn't want to hear him tell me all about the basket of cute kittens he saved on the way to the airport. At the rec center, I strolled to the back and found Darryl. His little command center was empty this time, so I just took the seat next to him and told him about my evening with Voss—Charlie—minus the sexy parts.

"I didn't say it before, because I didn't want to jinx it, but part of your mission was to even confirm our theories about the existence of magic-users. Mages, as it were. So, there's that done."

I sat up in my comfortable office chair.

"Wait...you weren't even sure? Seriously? I stalked an operator—a friend for weeks over a guess. What if you had been wrong?"

"My hunches, post-Supercell, have usually turned out right. But this was magic. Who could ever be one hundred percent certain?" I sighed. I guess it was too late to be as mad about this as I want to be. I didn't have the energy for it anyway. "But now that we know we're on the right track, we've got to find a way to stop our enemies."

"I've given that some thought on the flight back here," I said.

"What do you have?"

"The same shit we did with Voss. I think we can pull the same job twice. Use what we know to create a trap for them that they think is a trap for us. Tell me about the research you've done so far on The Imperative."

"Well, I've studied all of their probable interventions over the last two decades. Kazi and I both have. We know which kinds of policies provide them with benefit. We know which types of assets they are most often seeking to protect. We know at which stage of the decision-making process they usually hit."

"Exactly! So whip up something that gives us a list of possible strike points. All we've got to do is throw a monkey wrench in their gears and wait for them to show up to repair the machine. And that's where I come in," I said. "Ready to pick these guys apart and clear the way for our own." Darryl started typing. No doubt he was putting together some algorithm or running simulations on how best to disrupt The Imperative.

I was about to ease back into the chair and settle in for a nap when I had a disturbing thought. What made this different? This whole Phase Two plan sounded great, but it got started by taking agency away from Marcella and me. Our ability to choose it as a viable path was taken away from us. It's still being taken away from Marcella, with my help this time. So, how could we be sure that weren't denying agency to everyone that this plan ultimately effects? How did we know we're not just The Imperative, Part 2? "Hey, Darryl? Do you ever worry that you're just replacing one shadow government for another?"

"Not even for a second," he responded immediately, not bothering to look up from his screen. "Firstly, our people will be in front of the cameras, not skulking behind the scenes. There will be accountability for us: public servants with names and faces that people can find with an internet search or engage on social media. Secondly, we're trying to help people. We aren't just looking after our own self-interests." He lifted his fingers from the keyboard and turned to face me. "Look, regardless of our team and our goals, The Imperative is bad news. They aren't just holding power to themselves; the changes they're making are a foot on the throat of the public. People are dying as a result. I'm not talking about rich prats who can afford the services of an operator. I'm talking about poor folks who can't afford homes or meds because the markets have been stacked against them. The Imperative is oppressive. Thirdly, unlike you, I plan to eventually leave the shadows and step into the light where I can get some recognition for my good deeds. Hence the rec center."

"Yeah, I was gonna ask you about that. What's the deal with this place?" I asked. Darryl's face broke into a huge smile. He'd been waiting to talk about his passion project. But first he looked to his computer, minimized the window he was working on, and began searching for a specific directory of files.

"Kani and Mark are out in the field with the folks they intend on serving. Even Kazi has his gaming cons full of adoring fans and eager groupies. I needed to be near the people I was trying to assist. Real people. I didn't want to lose touch of our focus. So, I reopened this

131

place and poured a bunch of money into it." He paused to turn a monitor in my direction. It showed a map of Columbus with a shifting cascade of gradient colors. I was too tired to make immediate sense of what I was looking at. But Darryl was excited, so I just let him finish explaining himself. "It's made a huge difference too. A lot of the people we serve here are affluent local residents. But even more of them are neighborhood kids with nowhere better to be. They mix and mingle here and get a better idea of each other's humanity in the process. Take a look! Not only has the crime rate dropped in the city, but diversity in local businesses has gone up—all in the six years since we've open. And the remaining crime in the city happens everywhere except here. The area gangs have named the rec center a no-fly zone for violence. This place is Switzerland. When all of this is over, maybe I'll put my real name on the front." These were the real answers I needed to hear. It was a good plan. All of this was. Phase Two was shaping up and I was glad to be a part of it. I just...wish Marcie was here with me. She was the last thing I thought about before drifting off.

"Sana, wake up. We're back on."

I don't know how long I was out, but I was on the wrong side of refreshed.

"What's happening?"

"I've come up with a list of business and initiatives that are likely points of protection for The Imperative. If we target any one of these, there should be a response that we can exploit. As you're the business end, it's really up to you to decide which tact to take." He handed me a stapled packet of four sheets of paper.

Flipping through the papers, I saw that it was a directory of several companies and bills and the information behind each. "There's a lot of names here."

"Yeah. It's shocking to see how much reach they have. And these are just the points we could track."

"It's also shocking to see just how overconfident they are. For such a small group wielding such incredible power, they've left so many weak points exposed here. Weak points they didn't think anyone might ever spot or exploit."

"I hadn't really thought about it that way."

"That's why I'm the operator here, Darryl." It was easy to get lost in the dozens of entries here. "Okay, I see the names and the info but what does it mean to target any of these things?"

"Well, someone would need to put their hands over the faucet in any of these cases. Someone would need to try to shut down one of these fake projects or divert funding away from these fake companies."

"Someone like who though? Who has the ability to make those kinds of changes?" I said.

"The executives of any of the competing companies, really. If they demand a chunk of that government budget or if they put out a better product, The Imperative would have to take notice. Hell, they don't even have to really do any of that. From this room, we can fabricate the documents that would make it appear like they are."

133

"Stop right there. You're talking about creating a patsy. I've done that before, made people think that money was moving, or people were saying things that they weren't. It's a good move if you're trying to cause chaos. But we're trying to create a clear path to a target that we designate. Then we, which is to say I, must be waiting on that path to make an interception. It's a messy play, Darryl. We're not The Imperative. We don't control any of these people. They could immediately contradict any fabricated documents that we put together. Which, again, is great if we're sowing chaos. But that's not what we're doing. Also...it's unethical. I know I'm maybe the last person who should be haggling about ethics, but whoever the target is should be wearing a jersey. Someone in the game. Not just someone in the stands who gets pulled onto the field."

"That's completely fair. If we're sticking to the resources we've got available, there's always Mark. When he wins his election, he could reasonably lean on most of items on the list."

I thought it over for a minute, then shook my head. "True, but by that time, The Imperative could know they have some competition. They might respond unpredictably to knowledge of our presence. We should maximize how much we can accomplish before that election goes down." I thumbed the list looking for something specific.

"We can always come back to utilizing Mark as an asset later, since the election is going down regardless of what we do next."

"What about this one here?" I pointed the directory to Darryl and tapped my finger on an entry. He broke into a smile, rolled back over to his computer, and started typing.

"That'll work. Let me mock something up really quick." Most of the entries on the list were agriculture companies and fueling solutions. A politician could interfere, but we didn't have a politician on staff yet. At least, not a working or influential one. An entry for Barlowe Labs is one of few listed as a pharmaceutical company. We may not have had a politician, but we did have the foremost talent in medical science. The plan didn't take long to form.

"I've got it," Darryl said. "The wheels were already greased on this one. All right, so working backwards, Dennard Medical has a liver damage drug on the market. It has government backing and runs about twelve dollars per pill. A large share of the proceeds go to a figurehead that doesn't exist. Whenever someone makes a stink about the ridiculous price, the politicians try to funnel money to a rival company, Barlowe, which claims to be researching a seven dollar generic version of the same drug. When you investigate their R&D department, the money goes to a similar nonexistent figurehead. In her free time, our girl Kani has developed a far more effective medicine that will retail at just under fifty cents per pill. It's been relatively low priority against the other work we've done but, if she pushes it to the right people, the Imperative will have to respond or lose both revenue streams."

I bristled at her being referred to as "our girl." I wasn't ready yet to let that part of the past go, given that it had been the worst for Marcie. I pushed the anger down.

"So, let me guess," I said. "She gets this new drug out to market and we appear when the enemy arrives to course correct?"

"No. Not quite. If she puts her work in the hands of the politicians, the Imperative will alter them. So, we just need her to reveal the drug and gather support without actually making any official moves to getting the drug it's taxpayer funding."

"That way the only way to stop the buzz is to stop Kani herself." The plan was simple enough. We just had to set our stage. "Contact Kani and have her create a routine out of her day. Something easy to track. Something that ends her day in the same simple trap of a location. We want our prey to think they've got the upper hand...until they don't."

"Well, you're the strategist, love. Maybe you can talk to Kani and—"

"No." I wasn't ready to hear her voice yet. "Figure it out, according to your plan, and give me my window of opportunity." If Darryl wanted to believe everything was forgiven, that was his fantasy. I wasn't willing to play along.

Chapter Thirteen

"There are members of the board who disputed my recent appointment and I wanted to address that. The idea that I'm arrogant comes from two places. Firstly, my age. Secondly, my demand for independence to work apart from some of the board's goals. Essentially, I'm too young to accomplish all the things that I've already accomplished. To protect the egos of those older than me, I should downplay that my recent breakthroughs have eclipsed theirs. And to further avoid bruising those egos, I should shackle myself to the ideas and methodology of a board that doesn't always work as efficiently as it could for those that it serves. Please understand, I greatly value the contributions of those who came before me, but I'm not here to kiss any rings. I'm here to help the most people in the best ways. If that's your goal as well, then we shouldn't have any problems."

— *Dr. Kani Sidana, on her addition to the Medical Board of America*

She knew...but she didn't. Kani couldn't see me anywhere, but she knew I was everywhere. She understood that the plan called for me to follow her, to observe, and to familiarize myself with the environment. But I was a professional, so I was nearly invisible for the entire process. It had been weeks. It had to be unnerving. I hoped that it was unnerving. It was unnerving for me.

Seeing her brought back a flood of memories that I didn't want. Kani had been the responsible one on our project. She made sure we were all sleeping and eating regularly. Though her brother usually picked the activity, it was her who always suggested when we took breaks. She's the reason we called our nanotechnology "Supercell" in the first place. It was a kind of generic name, but it perfectly matched up with her proposed idea of mapping biological functions to technological ones. It changed the trajectory of the project entirely. I owed her for the long-running success of my very best work. I also owed her for being part of one of the first tests to my and Marcella's then-new relationship.

Even though Marce had told me she would neither adhere to nor burden me with notions of exclusivity, I still felt like I had cheated on her the first time I slept with Mark. When I told her about it the following morning, it was a tear-streaked confession. She was completely unfazed. Not only had Marcella casually added that she had also been sleeping with Mark, she offered up a high-five, and congratulated me for my "first time with a guy." Then she expected a high-five in return for hooking up with Kani the night before. No tears. No confession. Just the matter-of-fact sharing of good news. That was Marcella all over. No walk of shame. Just a stride of pride. A got-laid parade. Ugh! I was such an asshole about it. I went from feeling like a betrayer to feeling like the betrayed over the course of about sixty seconds. The hypocrisy!

It's memories like those that I wanted to be able to laugh and joke about. I wanted to hold all of it dear as fun reminders of where we all came from. But, with our last meeting, I didn't see the woman who took care of us or improved my tech or had fun times with my favorite person. All I saw was the person who treated us so callously while we were already struggling to understand why we'd been abandoned. Even before she was Double M, Marcella had a sort of above-it-all invincibility to her. Pain and crisis usually just shook away like water off a duck's back. I'd only really seen her seriously hurt a few times. That dismissal was one of those times. And now I had to watch almost every move of the person who did the dismissing? It was frustrating to say the least.

Each morning, I started my day just before sunrise. Kani set herself up at the Four Seasons hotel in the Georgetown area of Washington, D.C. She wasn't comfortable using her home in nearby Silver Spring, Maryland, as the basis for an operation. I couldn't blame her. There's no telling what kind of collateral damage we might produce. Plus, it was easier to see the patterns in a city as highly scheduled as our nation's capital. Between the politicians, the tourism, twenty colleges, and a tightly run mass transit system, it felt like everybody was on a deadline. You could almost set your watch by the movements of individual residents, Kani being one of them.

At seven-fifteen, she would leave the hotel every morning for her daily run up and down the waterfront. According to her, the isolation and focus of her runs were the source of some of her best ideas. She didn't need the workout, given the nanites in her system.

139

That hour was one of the few times each day where she was outdoors without me shadowing her. With the tech in her body, she was lightning fast. About twelve miles cleared each morning. She could win a marathon at any level. Of course, I could easily keep up with her, but I'd have to break cover to do so. Two elite-class runners jogging along the Potomac within a few seconds of each other every morning would raise eyebrows. I also didn't think there was any chance of The Imperative approaching her out there. So I was fine just spending that time gathering info about the area surrounding the hotel. The part where I gathered information about Kani would start when she returned.

What I discovered during the fact-finding portion of this op was that I was already familiar with Kani. When she arrived at her office, a remote working space near Union Station, she pulled the curtains and the windows all the way open. Every single day. Even when it was cold or rainy. She always needed to be closer to flowing air and natural light. It had made working in that basement lab so difficult as teenagers. There were days where she dragged her chair outside and worked away from the rest of us—far enough from the house to be in the sun, but close enough that her laptop still connected to the WiFi. That need, those open windows, also made it easy to spy on her corner office from my post at a nearby park.

Darryl arranged an extension of the chirp line for Kani to use. While we didn't communicate directly, I used the line to listen in on her phone calls and interoffice chatter. She even sounded the same. Not just her voice, but how quickly she spun herself into hard-to-follow medical jargon when discussing her work. Luckily, she had far more opportunities to speak to other experts in her field. I'm glad she finally found people who understood what she was talking about. That's something Marcella and I always had each other for.

During more casual conversations with the people in her office, her irreverent tone was exactly what I remembered. Right down to certain phrases she still used.

"Thank goodness you're on-site today, Dr. Sidana. You won't believe what happened to me this weekend," a coworker blurted out while rushing into Kani's office.

"God, Diane! Nobody cares who you fucked!"

The two women burst out laughing before Diane began retelling the boring tale of a home improvement project gone wrong.

Neither of them could hear me, but I laughed right along with them. Kani had said those exact words to me at least a dozen times. I'd heard her say it even more to Marcella. The more things changed, the more they stayed the same, I guess.

Like the things she ate. For lunch, she still preferred total junk. Cheese fries, chili dogs, and extra-large soft drinks. It was one of the only things she really had in common with her brother.

The only real difference that struck me hard were her clothes. When we met in high school, she'd tended to wear frumpy, baggy clothes. She'd always been gorgeous, but unfortunately her beauty inspired a lot of unwanted attention from asshole high school boys. Her new personal style was made up of below-the-knee dresses that were both professional and comfortable, neither hiding nor accentuating her curves. It seemed her wardrobe was no longer chosen based on external forces. Good for her.

Part of watching Kani was seeing her manage the tedious aspects of her job. As one of the foremost experts in the medical industry, she made a considerable salary as an independent consultant. This meant several hours of dealing out career-fixing and product-improving advice. And, of course, broadcasting her development of a formula for Amaxane, the drug to replace Desarall on the market. Most of that consisted of phone calls to politicians and administrators. Boring for sure, but it was an incredible and disheartening window into the inner workings of the medical industry. Kani had to argue passionately to receive support for her new drug. Medicine that does a better job and costs a ton less shouldn't even need an argument. But there we were. There was a magic to listening to her turn the hearts of the heartless.

The kind of magic I was most interested in—the kind like Charlie's—came into play when a call came from a gentleman with a booming voice seeking to set up a meeting.

"Good evening, Dr. Sidana. My name is John Hale. I'm a lobbyist for several pharma firms. I've got to say I'm a huge fan of your work. The safer helmets you developed for pro football have made the game so much less of a guilty pleasure for me. But anyway, my clients see a bright future for your new liver damage drug, Amaxane, and think our support could really carry some weight in making it available to the right people. I'd like to get some time on the calendar where I could drop by your office and discuss possible distribution and pricing options."

"Hale? You said your name was Hale?" I picked up my binoculars just in time to see Kani start to lose her composure. We only gave her a limited stack of information on the people we were after. Just names and basic physical descriptions really. Much more than that might've changed the way she acted and possibly tipped off The Imperative. The plan had me doing all the heavy lifting as far as interacting with the enemy. She hadn't considered the possibility that she'd be speaking to them directly. None of us had. We'd been managing this play the way we had with Voss. We weren't prepared for a public-facing target.

"Yes. John Hale. Would it be possible to schedule some time to discuss the future of Amaxane?"

"I... ummm...Could you hold on a moment? I don't want to...lose my train of thought. Let me get a note down."

Kani was a lot of things, but she wasn't an operator. She wasn't used to improvising under pressure. From my position, with my binoculars, I could see her stand up and begin to pace. I had to break my silence to step in. I lightly tapped the button on my touchpad to bring myself to an audible volume. "Stay calm, Kani. Just apologize to him. Tell him that your office schedule is full but you can gladly meet him tonight...at the hotel. Invite him to the trap."

She reacted with a start. It took her a second to place my voice, but when she did, she looked out the window. She couldn't see me, of course. She was just guessing at where I was, and her gaze was far to the left of my actual location. But maybe it made her feel a bit safer just knowing I was near. She took a deep breath and slowly said, "My apologies, Mr. Hale. I just checked my schedule. Unfortunately, due to some upcoming travel, my office hours appear to be booked for quite a while. At least for the next three weeks. I may have some time tonight though, if you don't mind being a bit informal."

"What did you have in mind, Dr. Sidana?"

"I'm currently staying at the Four Seasons in Georgetown. Do you know it?"

"I do, yes."

"I've got an event to attend at nine. If you meet me in room 426 at eight, I can give you half an hour while I get myself ready for it. I know it's a bit unorthodox. But it's either that or wait a month for my office hours to be free. By that time, Amaxane may have all the support it needs." She spoke calmly but covered the phone's receiver and broke into deep panicked breaths between exchanges. Maybe she had it in her after all.

"It is unorthodox. But I've had productive meetings under strange circumstances before. I'll see you tonight."

"Great. Thank you. See you then." Bravo, Kani. This thing finally panned out. I had a few hours of lead time to get back to the Four Seasons and make sure we maintained the upper hand we'd worked so hard to establish.

Chapter Fourteen

"There isn't really a community for operators. That sucks. The superheroes are damn near as competitive as we are. But they also talk to each other. They share resources, attend conventions, visit each other's cities, and team up. Operators rarely do any of that. Most times we don't even know each other's locations or specialties. We can't offer referrals to our friends in the industry since most of us don't have any. Someone needs to get on that."

— *Operator Andy* — For Hire *magazine* — *July 2017*

Darryl had left his rec center to join us in Washington DC. He'd be providing on-site op support. It was a new role for him, but he wanted to be "in the field" for this one. If he did what I needed him to do, I didn't have a reason to tell him to stay on the bench.

We had arranged a routine for Kani that left her about two hours a day of time by herself in the room we had lined up. It was supposed to appear to be a window of opportunity for anyone that might've sought a private word with her. The problem was, we hadn't been expecting actual words to occur.

With Hale accepting an invitation to the room, we could change the play a little bit. I didn't have to hide in the adjoining room during that window of opportunity, waiting for a strike. Instead, I'd arrive alongside Hale, posing as room service. When the hotel's camera feeds were reviewed after the op, Kani wouldn't look like an accomplice. She'd look like an unwilling witness. She could call the authorities after I'd left, then feed them any narrative we want.

Each night, during our reconnaissance, Darryl would hang out near the hotel lobby bar with a drink and a laptop tapped into the building's security. He'd been my eyes and ears. Not that there'd been anything to see before then. I quietly waited in the adjoining hotel room dressed as a server, complete with a rolling cart. As soon as I heard anything from the room or from Darryl, I would slip into action.

Chirp

"Are you ready, Sana? It's about to go down," Darryl said.

"Well yeah. I know what time it is," I responded. "Do you see something in particular?" This was the first time he'd spoken to me, over the earpiece, with anything but idle chatter. That made it harder to get into the right headspace. I would remember that in case I needed to work with someone else again. No bad habits.

"Well, three people fitting the descriptions you got from Voss just showed up to the bar. An older, dark-haired woman in a suit, a tiny Latina in baggy clothes with...chunky jewelry, and a hench black fellow also in a suit. All heavily tattooed on the few bits of skin I can see showing. They're ordering drinks. Having a good night apparently."

"The overconfidence there is stunning. Meeting and having drinks in public? Like they've got nothing at all to hide." I shook my head. "I'm half-astonished and half-impressed. Let me know if anything changes."

It would be about half an hour before it did. "The fellow is on the move, Sa. Heading towards the elevators with a walking stick."

"That's Hale. I'm on it." I slipped open the door to my room and pushed out my dining cart to face in the direction of Kani's room. Timing would be essential here, so I began to take several steps backwards away from both of our rooms to create space equidistant from the elevators on the opposite side. When the elevator reached the fourth floor, a chime sounded. That's when I slowly made my way towards the target room just as Hale did the same from the opposite direction. The walking stick that Darryl mentioned had become a large and ornate staff. Maybe there was a sort of glamour magic that he used in more public spaces. He wasn't bothering to keep it hidden or disguised from the service worker walking towards him from the far end of the hallway. That didn't bode well.

Though I had an on-the-job alias, I almost never wore a mask when I worked. Why bother? I didn't have much of a public life that I needed to protect and being an operator wasn't like being a superhero. Sure, I had a small photo of my face appear in the *For Hire* rankings each month, but there were no public records of the deeds I'd had done to get there. There were no JC media appearances, no JC fan clubs, and no JC commercials selling JC modeled action figures. I barely got noticed at Luke's Lockup and I was there a few times a week. Even if someone recognized me from that single photo, there probably wouldn't be much of a reaction...unless I showed up in a strange circumstance. Like, say, in a hotel right outside the door of someone you meant to brainwash.

Simple recognition wasn't my only concern though. This would be the first of three targets, all of whom I was told I'd be outclassed by. The stakes of failure would be the lives of people I've known since high school. A single flip-through of our high school yearbook would connect me to the woman in that hotel room, her twin brother, and a soon-to-be popular politician. Anyone who figured that out would probably make the next leap to spot that I grew up one town over from Double M and that we're the same age. For the first time in my career, my secret identity became a concern. So... I wore a mask, untied my hair, and hung my head low.

In the dimness of the hallway, I wasn't expecting the taller man to pick up on the fact that the server walking towards him had a covered face. He didn't. I also wasn't expecting him to notice me taking my right hand off the cart as he knocked on Kani's door. He wouldn't. I pulled level with Hale just as the door opened. I was only a step past him when, from the holster on my right thigh, I drew my long knife and drove it into his back with a high arching backhand. Right side central. Enough to knick his lung and leave him spluttering, but not enough to kill.

What I was expecting was for natural human instinct to spin him around to see who his attacker was. But Kani opened the door at just the wrong second. The momentum of my strike pushed him into the room and his staff acted like a cudgel and knocked her unconscious.

Fortunately for me, Hale's two-handed grip on his staff was tight and strong. It was just like a martial arts student holding up a wooden board for their teacher. Or at least that's what I was thinking as I punched directly through it. The next punch broke his nose and folded him right up, leaving him unable to focus on anything but those multiple points of pain.

I looked down at her. It was the first time we'd been in a room together in years. Her knocked out on the floor and me whipping out a silenced pistol while standing over a bleeding man? Not really the most ideal reunion. I kicked the door closed then held my gun level with his chest. He was done. "We need to talk. Now. Before you bleed out."

"You don't know what you're in the middle of here. I'm not just some corporate shill. You're fucking with shit way out of your league." His voice was raspy and stuttering.

"I know, Hale. I know. You're going to tell me all about The Imperative...assuming you want to see the light of another day." His eyes went wide. He wasn't expecting me to know the name.

Chirp

It was Darryl. Couldn't answer that now. And now Hale is laughing. Great. Intimidation failed.

"You picked the wrong contract this time, operator."

Chirp

Seriously, Darryl needed to stop. I was in the middle of a... And that's when I saw it. Just over the white collar of Hale's shirt was the corner of a tattoo. A glowing tattoo. Hale had never fully let go of his

149

broken staff. I didn't know what kind of functionality he could get out of that thing, but I wasn't going to wait to find out. I put two bullets in his chest and one in his head. One down. Two to go. Then I tapped the touchpad for my communicator.

In my earpiece, Darryl was halfway into a sentence. He was almost yelling now. "—to leave right away. Sana, come in. Jace fucking Clementine, can you hear me? It's time to go, if you haven't already! The other two are on their way up. They look like they know what's happening up there. I'm heading to the rendezvous point." Shit! I closed the line without bothering to respond.

I didn't know what that tattoo said but obviously it was some sort of failsafe or a signal. With Kani unconscious and the other two mages on their way, there was no time to leave the way we had planned. Time to improvise. I holstered the sidearm, retrieved my knife, and whipped out my phone. I always kept the Supercell app open when I'm on the job just in case the situation changed up from under me. Like right then and there. I swiped over to my Favorites and chose the pre-programmed "Double M" configuration.

I could feel the difference immediately. I went from feeling lighter than air to feeling denser than steel. At first, it was the feeling of a weighted blanket or a strength training vest. Disorienting to start but then everything around me started to feel flimsier. Less substantial. This is what Marcella felt like all the time. As if the world itself might break at her touch. She programmed her own favorite configuration into my phone years ago. "Just in case you need to be heroic one day," she'd said with a wink and that big smile. She never stopped taking care of me.

The settings controlled the nanites, but also the armor I was wearing. Based on existing hover tech, I had created a modified magnetic levitation system limited to just a few inches. To my feet, it would feel like I was still grounded. In reality, I'd be silently standing, running, or walking on thin air. Marcie adapted it to her armor to allow for anti-gravity jumps. She couldn't fly like an airplane, but she could take off and land like one.

As my work usually required softer hands, I'd never had a reason to use the change in settings before. It was time to see how the other half lived.

I reached down and pulled Kani up by her arm and slung her over my back in a fireman's carry. I had to take extra care not to yank her shoulder out of its socket with my unexpected new strength. The room's windows were divided by a frame that allowed guests to slide one side open to let the breeze in. For us, it was just in the way. I punched through the glass, gripped the frame, and ripped it down into the room. If I had another second to think, I'd have used the damaged frame as a barricade, because the hotel room door burst open just as I had built up a running start and charged towards the huge hole where the window used to be.

A glance to my right and I saw both Circe and Araña entering the room, tattoos glowing. I could see the air around Circe shimmering. The shimmer was gathering to a focal point: the baton in her hands. She was charging up to attack. Next to her, Araña's chains were streaming out of her sleeves and forming a pentagram, seemingly on their own. The charge around her gathered far faster and, by the time I had leapt through the window, I was immediately followed by an explosive blast of fire and ash.

Between my jump and the concussive wave that trailed it, I flew through the night air to the brick-faced building on the other side of 29th Street. There were no ledges to grab, so I gripped deep into a flat vertical wall. The last-minute adjustment to my Supercell technology left my skin and muscles extra dense. I might as well have been digging my fingers into a flaky pie crust. It would slow our descent and allow me to make an anti-gravity padded jump down to street level before our pursuers could give chase. Despite the config change, the hardware specific to my armor just didn't have the same array of inertial dampeners that Double M's had. So the landing was rougher than expected but it served to jostle Kani awake. I looked up to the fourth floor and saw Circe and Araña staring down at us. Now we just had to hope they didn't lob any more fireballs at us before we got our bearings.

Chapter Fifteen

"Talking to superheroes is easy! Most celebrities have a product to sell. A movie, a show, an album, whatever. Even if they're a terrible guest, they'll show up and be terrible. Not heroes, though. They're only trying to sell themselves. Either they've got a ton of personality and make for a great interview or they're not interested in fame and don't show up at all. Most of the boring superhumans are too low key to show up on my radar. Or they become operators."

— *Talk show host Shae Livingston on* Morning Gab — *May 2012*

"Can you run?" I said to Kani. I knew she'd recover quickly. Her enhanced physiology made that a guarantee. But I didn't need her to recover quickly. I needed her to recover immediately. Otherwise, I had to put her back over my shoulder, which would change our escape a little bit. She was clearly still disoriented, but she nodded her head, kicked off her wedges, and gathered them up in her hands. I switched my nanites back to my usual settings. I wanted to feel like I was back in my own body before we headed off into the night.

The initial plan was for Kani to stay and feed misinformation to the police about Hale's death. I would sneak down the stairs to the parking garage and meet Darryl there. We'd escape and Kani would go back to work the next day. Like it never happened. But that was the quiet plan. With Kani unconscious and with no way of telling what kind of information Hale passed to his partners before I shot him, there was no way I could have left her there. Not while assuring her safety. This was magic we were talking about. Circe and Araña could've done anything to her. Tortured her. Killed her. I had literally no idea. She had to go out that window with me.

Once everything went big and loud, we had to change out to Plan B. If I couldn't make it to the parking garage within five minutes of the call to evacuate, we were to meet near the Lincoln Memorial within the following 30 minutes. I don't know exactly when the clocks started. Either the five-minute evacuation clock or the 30-minute rendezvous clock. But it didn't matter. From the sound of Darryl's frantic voice over the chirp line, he was skipping over the evac plan. I understood why. He wanted to be gone as quickly as possible and, with The Imperative closing in, it would've been reckless for me to try to reach him in the parking garage.

As for the rendezvous point, the Lincoln Memorial was just over a mile away. About half an hour to walk. But a pair of world class runners, like us, could clear the distance in less than ten minutes; that was even with me slowing down so Kani could keep up. Had this been rush hour, we would have beaten Darryl's car to the meeting spot. We had more than enough time to hit that deadline.

Following my lead, Kani and I cut back across the same 29th Street we just flew over. Right next to the hotel was a short trail that led behind it and over to Rock Creek and Potomac Parkway. Once we got to the side of the hotel, we'd be out of the mages' line of sight. From there, we'd take a jogging path along the riverwalk until we hit the edge of the National Mall...and our goal. We both knew the game plan, so talking wasn't really necessary, in my opinion. Kani didn't see it that way.

"Sana, I just wanted to say thank you. For the save back there and for the assist talking to Hale. I couldn't have gotten through either without you." She wasn't out of breath yet, but there was still a shudder to her voice. Fear or anxiety maybe. Didn't matter.

"Mm-hmm..." I said. I didn't even look at her. I just kept running. We weren't out of danger. The Supercells had kept her in excellent condition. Because of them, she could keep up with me a lot easier than almost anyone else I might run with. But I was considering picking up speed just to avoid a conversation.

"After all this time...I didn't know how this was going to play out. I've never been on either end of that sort of...operation. Tonight, I feel like I was on both." It was nervous energy. She was wound up after experiencing some exciting shit. Back in the day, Marcella would've had a cure for that. Right there and then? She needed to work that energy out some other way. Lucky for her we were running. I hoped she'd run it off without me needing to engage at all.

"Yeah," I responded, hoping she would pick up on my reluctance to chat.

"I should've known it would all shake out just fine. You are the top operator on the list, right? At least before you joined up for Phase

Two." Bringing up my fall in the power rankings wasn't going to make this more pleasant for either of us.

"Right." Seemed like there was only one way out of this. She was speaking between labored breaths now as I picked up the pace slightly.

"Something else I wanted to say..." Great. Here it comes. "I'm so sorry for how I treated you and Marcella the last time we saw each other. I know it was part of the plan and I know that you understand that now. But it was really hard for me and I'm sure it was really hard for the two of you as well. I've agonized over it ever since and..."

"Enough!" I pulled out of my run to a complete stop. We weren't even a quarter mile from the memorial, but I couldn't let this go on a single second longer. Professionalism be damned. I pointed a finger to her chest, stopping just short of a poke, and said, "There were so many ways you could've handled that situation and you picked the worst one. I don't need to hear about how hard it was on you. I don't need to hear anything at all. Not now. We are literally running for our lives here. Let's just get where the fuck we're going. Quietly!" I felt shitty right after I said it. Her voice was trembling the whole time she spoke. Her whole body was. Whether it was nervous energy or not, she had been waiting to say that for years. Probably since the day after we last met. Ugh! All these stupid feelings. I didn't need this right now. Or ever.

The rest of the run went without any further dialogue. There was the occasional sniffle that indicated that Kani might've been crying,

156

but I didn't bother to check. Darryl was already waiting, parked in a rented car, by the time we reached the monument. I climbed into the backseat, behind him as Kani got in the front. "All good, ladies?" I said nothing. Kani just gave Darryl a look that he seemed to understand before she pointedly looked out the passenger-side window. I pretended not to see.

With Kani being quite recognizable and her hotel room literally blowing up behind us, we decided to drive the seven to eight hours from DC to the rec center in Ohio. Even though we quickly got out of their sight, we had no real way to gauge our enemies' capabilities in the immediate. Would they have access to all the city's resources to find us? If so, how soon? All we knew is that major travel centers for buses, trains, and airplanes were all about to be too dangerous. To avoid the possibility of facial recognition, Darryl's reconnaissance gave us a path out of the nation's capital with a bare minimum of traffic cameras. We already had a rental car under an assumed name. The safest move was a road trip. With stops for food and gas, we expected to arrive back in Columbus just before sunrise.

With the radio on, we quickly learned the repercussions of tonight's actions. It was the top story on every station. The Imperative had unbelievable reach. The spin was lightning fast and it came directly from the police commissioner. Hale was being identified as John Christopher Hale, a lobbyist for "several large pharmaceutical agencies," none of which were named. The news media was already speculating that his death was a politically motivated murder centered around expensive government contracts combined with sloppy use of an operator. A proper contractor would've performed the hit without any witnesses or collateral damage. So I was being blamed for the explosion as well. Great!

Had this been a real contract, filed and accepted, malpractice on this scale would've been traced back to Darryl and myself. We'd be arrested and indicted for the damage we'd done to both civilians and businesses. But this wasn't a real contract. Technically, I wasn't even an operator for any of this. Without proof of legitimate employment, I was a rogue. The mages had to know that. As well connected as they were, the operator database would've been the first thing they checked. Maybe a rogue operator would cause more of a public panic than they could reasonably control, especially because Kani was now being reported as kidnapped by an operator. The same one she was seen flying out of a hotel room with. Game developer Kazi Sidana was also wanted for questioning as a person of interest.

"That's definitely a slip up," Darryl said, mostly to himself, and I agreed. If Kani had really been kidnapped, there would be no reason to suspect her brother all the way out in California. But Circe and Araña saw us run off together. That, for them, meant a plot. And a detained Kazi could either be a lead to answers about that plot or an insurance policy against the plot's next steps. Or both.

I was impressed with how close to the truth they were able to stick. If Circe and Araña recognized me, they'd be able to track down my hometown and high school association with the Sidanas. If they didn't, there was still Mark. Once he got on the national scene, anybody with an internet search would be able to look up our graduating class and spot the young girl from the *For Hire* power rankings. As my name had yet to be mentioned in the news reports, I could only hope that I was still anonymous as anything other than "the operator."

The scariest part of the night was when the news reported law enforcement's attempted questioning of Kazi. His status rewarded him with soft treatment. The police arrived at his home to politely request that he come down to the station. The officers were later found unconscious with their car missing. The car was eventually recovered. Kazi was not. The report made Kani go quiet. I tried to give her a look, to maybe offer her some support. She didn't notice, and I resumed sitting quietly in the backseat.

Pulling into the rec center parking lot just before four in the morning, it struck me how lonely it felt. It was empty. I had begun to get used to seeing it bustling with activity. It would be another hour or so before the place opened, so Darryl had to use his keys to unlock the doors. We followed close behind, and I scanned the lot for any possible threats. I knew I didn't really have to worry, but the allegations of operator sloppiness had me bristling.

We didn't encounter any signs of life until we saw the illumination under the door to the command center. "Expecting company, Frost?" I said, using the alias to put him on alert.

"Absolutely not. Get ready!" He glanced at the knife on my thigh and drew it from its scabbard. Something about the action felt...intimate, companionable. I shook the feeling off.

It made more sense for me to take point, but Darryl left me behind him as he charged into his command center to find a half empty pizza box, a bottle of whiskey, several soda cans, and a sleeping Kazi Sidana drooling at a workstation.

Chapter Sixteen

"It's the most realistic military sim that you can fit on a small screen. We may or may not have had to tone down the realism to prevent gamers from waging war and overthrowing the government."

— *Kazi Sidana at Gameworld 2014 on his new game* Oath of Honor

"You cheeky bastard!" Darryl called out, startling Kazi awake. All tension gone from his body, he lobbed my knife back to me without looking. It reminded me of when Kazi had thrown his own pocket knife at me years ago, full-strength, to test my then-brand-new nanites. I easily caught the knife then too. Kazi had called it a test of my reflexes. What a dick.

In the present, Kazi almost fell out of the chair, but he still recovered his balance somewhat gracefully. He didn't deserve those nanites. "What the fuck are you yelling for, man? I'm the only one in here."

"Are you kidding?" Darryl threw up his hands. "We didn't know you were going to be here. I forgot you even had a key. How'd you get here? How'd you beat us here? On the drive in, we heard you disappeared."

"You wanna know how I disappeared? This is how!" Kazi leapt forward and started throwing soft punches at Darryl, who playfully dodged and parried each one, his anger dissipating. I rolled my eyes at the immaturity of it while simultaneously missing when Marcella would do the same. "When the cops came, I just CQC'd those fuckers and bounced! What's to explain?" He stopped punching and settled down a bit. "Seriously, from what I knew about the situation, what you told me about the play, and what I had heard about the escape, I knew the cops weren't really cops. I mean, maybe they were. But there was no way I'd ever get a fair shake, if they brought me in. I'd be in a windowless room somewhere getting tortured with magic. Which is kind of funny, if you think about it. What's that even look like? Maybe they'd pull rabbits out of hats or saw me in half or something until I gave up my secrets.

"Either way, I couldn't let that happen. The cops came in a single car. They thought I'd be a creampuff rich boy. So they never had their guard up. I put them down gently and skipped out. I've got a few friends who owe me favors. Friends with private jets. I'd have flown my own, but I knew they had to be watching my hangar."

"And you thought it wise to hide out here?"

"You can't KO the cops and then hang out at home. My shit is probably being investigated right now. All my gamedev buddies, including the one who let me borrow her jet, are gonna distance themselves from me. Nobody was gonna harbor me. I've got nowhere better to be. Plus, no one can trace us here. If I've got to be off-the-grid for a bit, might as well be amongst friends and in a place where I can help the cause. Hey sis!" Kazi smoothly disengaged from Darryl and gave his sister a kiss on the cheek and a hug she barely returned. He didn't really seem to notice. Maybe he was just used to half-hearted hugs from an exasperated sister.

"You see we've got an operator on site, Kaz?" Darryl called over as he walked over to his computer. Kazi looked over his sister's shoulder and spotted me standing away from the group.

"Hey you! Long time no see! Still looking fabulous, I see!" He ran over and gave me a big hug, lifting me up off the ground. Unlike with his sister, Kazi noticed and acknowledged my lack of enthusiasm in greeting him. "What's wrong? It's been like a decade and you don't hug me back?"

"We...didn't really have the best parting, Kazi." I murmured as he put me down and took a step back.

"I didn't believe it. Darryl told me that you were still mad at us, but I figured he had to be joking." As Kazi spoke, Kani joined Darryl and faded off to sit at a workstation. Apparently, both wanted to avoid whatever came next. I couldn't blame them. My reunion with Kani ended with me yelling at her. My reunion with Darryl started with a beat down. Still, I noticed they weren't skipping an opportunity to see it all unfold.

"Why would he be joking about that? What's funny about how I feel?" I also took a step back. Depending on where this went, I wanted room to take a swing.

"Umm...because us leaving was the best thing that ever happened to you," Kazi said while throwing his arms out like it was the most obvious thing ever.

"Excuse me? Explain how having eighty percent of my friends spontaneously bail on me is the best thing that's ever happened to me."

"You ungrateful bitch! We didn't bail on you, we set you free. We set you free while we shackled ourselves."

I gave him Marcie's Look.

"Sure, it looks nice now, but when the four of us left *that* basement dungeon of yours, Darryl and I crammed ourselves into *this* basement dungeon." I wasn't exactly okay with the lab where I spent most of my childhood being called a dungeon. It was one of the places I felt safest growing up. He wasn't doing himself any favors here.

"All of us took on obligations. Kani went to school. Darryl and I opened businesses. Mark got a real fucking job. He went from dating two hot geniuses to working at a factory in Nowhere, USA." He was pacing now and tugging at his hair. "I fucking employ people, Sana! I mean, so do Darryl, Mark, and Kani. But they're suited for that shit. I have meetings and make health insurance decisions and sort out interoffice disputes. There's a team of thirty developers who look to me as their boss. Me! They see me as the responsible one. And I guess I am, because I'm really worried about all of them right now. I don't know how my studio functions without me being on-site to rally the troops. But that's what I do daily.

164

"Meanwhile, you and Marcella spent the last eight years or so playing out your comic book action hero fantasies where she gets to be the good cop and you get to be the bad cop. Fighting and fucking and getting paid vast sums of money without being saddled with the burden of any real responsibility."

"It's not like that…" Ugh. It kind of was like that.

"The fuck it isn't!" He laughed. "How much money have you made as an operator? How much celebrity has Marcie gotten? You two are literally living the dream."

"We didn't do it for fame or for money."

"Yeah, well, then give all of it back. I know I could sure use a little more of each. Do you know how hard it is to keep from telling my employees that I know you two? Even as an operator, you're at least a minor celebrity and Double M is Double fucking M. In your respective fields you're both icons. The *For Hire* magazine ultimate secret power couple! And I'm sitting around pretending to be only vaguely familiar with either of you. Y'know one of my employees writes fan-fiction where she 'ships the two of you. Of course, she doesn't know that you're really together. So she gets it all wrong. Especially your personality. She's got you written as fun and outgoing and not a complete asshole. Pfft!"

"It hasn't all been action and excitement, Kazi."

"Oh I know…but a lot of it was! Darryl debriefed me about you catching and interrogating that operator. Voss13? Penthouse suites on the Vegas strip. VIP tickets to an Amazing Magisteria show with

165

backstage passes? Did you sleep with a Magisteria groupie? Oh my God! Did you sleep with Magisteria themself? Tell me you did. Please tell me you did and please make it be true."

Had I been living the dream? Why did I not feel that way, then?

"Hey, I get it," he said, moving forward, clapping a hand on my shoulder. "Once my game dev work took off and I got a little bit of notoriety, I started partying hard and sticking it to every fanboy who came my way. But we're all still living vicariously through you and Marcie."

"There's nothing that makes what you all did okay!" I pushed him away.

"You're right, you're right. And if you guys had walked out on me and my sister like that, we'd have been pissed off, too. But it wasn't just hard for you. You don't get exclusive rights to that shit. Mark fell into a depression without his two girlfriends. Kani didn't eat for two days after she was mean to you. I had to go to her campus and nurse her back to health. Feeding her liquified slices of pizza through a syringe. And Darryl's...well just look at him!"

"Fuck you!" Kani and Darryl both called over, no longer able to feign not eavesdropping.

"But it's been years," Kazi continued. "And, big picture, the only thing we did was get out of your way. We cleared a path for you to be exactly as awesome as you've been. You've had enough time to walk it off, now stop being a hardass and give me a real goddamn hug." I sighed...then I hugged my friend...and then I punched him in the gut. "I love you too, Sa," he said between clenched teeth.

"Yeah. It's good to see you again." He was right. It was time I let this shit go. All of it. It was either that or restart the anger/resolution process when I finally had a chance to talk to Mark directly. I would rather just be back at peace with the people I cared about.

I walked over to Kani and spun her chair around. "I'm sorry, Kani. Once I understood the circumstances, I should've forgiven you. I'm sorry I kept being a dick to you. We should've spent that whole drive catching up."

She looked me in the eyes plainly, not giving up much with her expression. It made me uncomfortable, but I deserved that. "You mean I should've spent the whole drive talking at you and you should've spent it being slightly less silent."

"Yeah. Basically. That." It was times like those that I wished I was better at expressing myself. Kani seemed to pick up on my difficulties. She stood up, smiled, and hugged me. It was a long and meaningful hug. The kind where lots of unspoken words are understood by both participants.

"Don't worry, Sa. I've already heard about a lot of your adventures. There'll be time for me to tell you all about mine."

"God, Kani! Nobody cares who you fucked." We both laughed. It felt good to have friends again.

Chapter Seventeen

"I don't discuss my powers, Matthew. You know that. And frankly, since you do already know that, I think it's rude that you keep asking. My powers, whatever they are, are an integral part of what makes me who I am. It's an invasion of privacy to keep hounding me about it. I've been really polite about it before, but you should seriously just knock it off."

— *Double M in* For Hire *magazine — August 2017*

A week had passed since the Hale operation. I woke to find Kani sitting at the edge of my bed. She was eating a bowl of cereal and reading something off a tablet computer. In the time since I took up residence here at the rec center, I still hadn't gotten entirely used to the beds in the dorms of the center's upper floors. On the other hand, I *had* already gotten used to waking up to these early morning status reports. This was the first time there in Columbus but it's exactly what Kani used to do when we worked on Team Supercell together.

I rolled from my back onto my stomach, in the direction of the bedside table, and reached out for the cup of coffee that I already knew would be waiting for me. A peace offering for the early wake-up. Lots of cream. Lots of sugar. She even remembered how I took it.

"Good," she said. "You're up. We've got good news and bad news. Come on downstairs and I'll get you up to speed." She stood up and held out a hand to me. I dragged myself to the edge of the bed and let her pull me up to standing.

She just as easily could've handed me a tablet or given me the details without removing me from a warm bed but Kani liked being around the rest of the team, especially her brother. Creating medical breakthroughs that aided the entire country was great, but Kani was just as comfortable playing Team Mom to our little squad. Plus, that allowed her to keep an eye on a brother—who she regarded as younger even though they were of course the same age. All that time in Washington, D.C. out of contact with the rest of us was difficult for her.

When we arrived back in the command center, Kani found a seat next to the workstation I usually claimed for myself. Darryl was in his usual spot to the left side of mine and Kazi was in the seat that mirrored my own on the other side of the room. I logged in and was immediately sent a link to the news. I clicked on it and was taken directly to an article dated for only a few hours earlier.

The headline read "United States Attorney General Declares War on Operators." I tapped the screen to play a video underneath the headline. An older white man in a suit was talking to an assembled group of reporters. "These criminals have worked on the fringes of the law for far too long. They are vigilantes and hired killers and the cold-blooded murder of lobbyist John Hale proves it. We will be tasking our country's community of law-abiding, officially-sanctioned superheroes with tracking down and taking down this scum once and for all! Any powered individual who takes up employment as an operator is being put on notice. Your days are numbered." He pounded his podium with each word of that last sentence. It felt like he was running for office.

"He sounds pretty serious. Should I be worried, Kani?" I stopped the video and looked over to her. She immediately began typing at her own terminal to bring something new on screen.

"Yes and no. Bobby Hollister is a bit of softy, as far as Attorney Generals go. I've met him a couple times in passing. Kind of a wet noodle. So if he's acting like this kind of a hardass, it means the Imperative is likely speaking through him. The president has already issued a statement of support. Normally this kind of move would require a lot of signed paperwork and voting sessions, but they've basically given Hollister emergency power to do whatever the fuck he wants. We think that means the president is enthralled as well. No politician would challenge this drastic of a measure for the sake of operators. They'd likely just let you all get snuffed out while protecting their own necks.

"The real worry, for us, is that this puts Marcella on the playing field. According to the article, the first phone call he made was to the Secret Service. The president offered one of the highest-ranking members to head up a special task force. The second call was to Double M, and she immediately accepted a position on that task force." Fuck! There was no telling what her involvement would bring. Double M was a wrecking ball. It's part of what I loved about her. She would fuck your plans all the way up with a big, beautiful smile and sexy—

170

I shook my head clear of the distraction. "You said there was good news?"

"Yeah. As you know, the rest of the team and I have been trying to secure all our lines of communication. That effort has finally extended to the private server where I keep all my personal research. I've got some breakthroughs on there that I've been perfecting for years. Stuff that'll enhance your Supercells...now that I have a genius-level tech babe here to help me finish it." I grinned at her. Forever ago, Marce and I joked about wanting "Genius-level Tech Babe" on our business cards. It was cute that Kani still remembered, but mostly I was just glad to have something to focus my energies on while I waited for the team to dig up any new information to help me find Circe and Araña.

"Let's see what you've got." Kani passed me her tablet and it was like an alternate reality version of that first day as teenagers when Marcella first handed me her design notebook. Then she...I really couldn't stop, could I? The more downtime I had, the more my head filled with thoughts of her.

The files on the tablet were full of brilliant ideas attached to shitty technology. Not extremely shitty. Just amateurish. That's why she needed me, though. Just like when we first made Supercell, I had to make the connection between biological functions and technological ones.

It would be a good distraction.

For the next two months, we hid out while the anti-operator task force took down every contractor they could find local to the Washington, D.C. area. My girl was unstoppable. Charlie knew it too, as The Amazing Magisteria called off the remainder of their American appearances and returned to Australia, citing a family emergency. Even though they weren't local to D.C., we all knew the task force would eventually go nationwide. That would put every one of us in the crosshairs. I wondered if their relationship could last through this. I hoped it would.

There were only ever five of us in the back room of that rec center now. Darryl and Kazi spent all their time running simulations, trying to create another trackable pattern of behavior for The Imperative. Kani and I revolutionized the Supercell's designs. And Ronnie was our gofer. The rest of Darryl's team of hackers were given financial bonuses and indefinite vacation time from the moment I became a fixture there.

The boys were sure they were on the edge of a breakthrough. Us girls were firmly entrenched in several breakthroughs. Along with some new medical tech for Kani, our redesigns netted us Supercells that could be localized to specific areas of the body and mapped to far more complex roles. My sight, my skin, my short-term and long-term memories—all were getting unbelievable new abilities. The biggest advancement was the connection of nanotechnology to neural pathways.

The app on my phone was going to be replaced with a comprehensive piece of software, written to a sub-dermal chip, and implanted at the base of my skull. All the new upgrades, as well as the old functionality, could be activated at will with an unparalleled level of control. The problem is that it was all on screen. On screen, it was perfect. But we didn't have a place to construct any of the components we'd gotten lined up. Not in Columbus, anyway.

That meant heading back to my mom's place. Kani wanted to come with me back to our old lab, back to our old town. She wanted to see my mother. I shot that idea down as soon as she spoke it. As far as we could tell, my identity was still a secret. Hers was completely public, especially in the place where we both grew up. There'd been a continuing search for her and Kazi for the last two months and there was no way home didn't have eyes on it. There was enough of a risk doing it myself, but it would be late at night when I arrived and the whole process should only take a few hours. I would get in, input all the new design specs, create the chip and a new set of nanites, then get out. I wouldn't even need to wake up Mom. Simple.

Until about three hours in, when Marcella arrived at the lab.

Chapter Eighteen

"The aspect of my training program that differs from what heroes get from their local stations is what I'm calling the 'Frank Curry Effect.' I want to make sure that trainees go back to their communities ready to fight crime, ready to fight injustice, and ready to build a platform to do both. We want to make sure that young heroes have as much power to create change as possible. Not just saving the day. But also saving the future."

— *Double M* — For Hire *magazine* — *July 2018*

It was my own fault. I would've already been heading back to Columbus if I hadn't spent some time creating something new for Kani. But I had that new gear in a case she provided and the sub-dermal chip sitting in an anti-static bag placed gently in my pocket. Only the nanites were left, the glass was in place, and I had just finished adding water to the fabricator. It would soon spit out a fresh batch of Supercells for me to ingest. It was just starting up when the door opened.

"Does your mother know you're here? I wouldn't want to wake her at this hour."

My heart started pounding. "Marcella." I was tired, but was I dreaming? How could she know I was at the lab?

"I still have a key to this place," she said with a small smile, reading me perfectly. I floundered, trying to decipher that smile. "I set up a camera and a motion sensor in here more than a month back, around when I first started hunting D.C.-area operators. When Kani and Kazi both vanished, I figured you must've been the one who killed John Hale and started this whole thing into motion. I got a ping on my phone the second you opened the door. Sorry it took so long to get here, but I was in Washington debriefing the Attorney General about my last catch. It would've been rude of me to skip out early. But, here we are. Are you ready to talk or are you ready to fight?" She was glad to see me, I was sure, but that could be as much about catching me as loving me.

"Can we think of a third option? I'm not really interested in fighting you...and you know how I am with talking." I tried to smile back. I failed.

"Yeah, I do know. You're only good at talking when you're lying to me." She took a step further into the room and let the door shut behind her. She'd described that to me before. It was a maneuver of hers: the pause at the threshold, the sharp statement, the door closing. It was all about intimidation, and I was surprised at how effective it was. She was on the job. I tensed.

"I told you I had something major to do. I told you I'd be hard to reach. What did I lie about?" I took a step closer to the fabricator as I spoke. It was a strategic choice, being next to some tech she wouldn't want to see damaged.

"You told me you were going off on a big contract. This isn't a job." She crossed her arms and waited for my response. I didn't understand where she was going with the statement.

"That's the truth."

"Explain it to me then. If this is a contract why have you fallen completely out of the top ten in rankings? Why are you targeting our high school friends? Why were you in Las Vegas fucking my partner behind my back?"

"None of that is what it looks like. Charlie and I—" Her eyes got wide and I immediately caught my own mistake. Fuck!

"So, they're 'Charlie' now? Not Magisteria, but *Charlie*," she said, making it sound like a curse. "Well, here's how it looks: You killed an innocent lobbyist and kidnapped two people we grew up with. You weren't contracted, you've gone rogue. You and Charlie have a secret relationship. Any corrections you'd like to make to those statements?"

"None of that is— Look, Marce, it's all really complicated. I can't really explain any of it." None of those statements were distinctly true or false. But I felt like shit for defaulting to the lack of transparency that had broken us apart in the first place. I wasn't ready for any this. Maybe I should have been.

"You don't have to," she said. "It's not like you'd tell me the truth anyway." She had lost her fake smile.

"How'd you find out about me and Charlie?" I said.

"About a couple hours after you lied to me about your 'mission-sensitive location.'" Her voice was mocking. I don't know that I'd ever heard it like this before, so bitter. It turned my stomach. "I turned on the TV to watch the live broadcast of Magisteria's twentieth anniversary special." I groaned audibly. Vegas is made of cameras. "I figured that if one of my loves was being sideways with me, maybe I could at least enjoy an honest version of another. Lo and behold, there you were, holding a queen of diamonds. You were visible a few other times during the show as well. You were even in the groupie seat."

"Wait, what?"

"Charlie puts their groupies in a specific reserved seat near the stage where they can be all sexy at them throughout the show. They did that with me before the first time we hooked up. Luckily, I had a big fan on their stage crew who warned me about it during the backstage after party. It was all balcony seats from then on."

She chuckled. I put a hand to my forehead and started chuckling as well. We both tried to stay reserved, but we couldn't help ourselves. It turned into the most honest laughter we've shared in years. When it finally died down, I saw Marcella wipe away a tear before sighing and moving on. "But when I called Charlie a week later to say I was worried about you, they acted like they hadn't seen nor heard from you since our threesome. And now they're running scared back to Australia citing a family emergency? They don't even *have* any family."

We're their family, I thought. *You and me*. But I couldn't say that, couldn't explain our connection without outing Charlie as an operator. "I don't know what to tell you, Marcella."

"Goddammit, Sana! Give me something. I can't just let you leave here. You're a rogue and a murder suspect."

"Nobody knows that except you, Marce."

"Yeah, but I *do* know it. My honor and reputation demand that I arrest you here and right now. You think I should just give you a pass?"

"Does it look like I'm over here appealing to your sense of mercy, O Great and Powerful M?" I was getting tired of her looking down on me and what I did. She couldn't stop me from leaving here even if that *was* her goal. Regardless of the rankings, I was the best operator in the game. Not that I had to be in this situation. "You couldn't arrest me if you wanted to, Double M. Your investigation is two and a half states away in Washington D.C. We're in New Jersey. We're not even in Cargill, where you probably still have city-wide jurisdiction. This is Rhodes. Even if I was guilty, you couldn't do shit about it."

"If I wanted to, Jace Clementine"—we both froze for an instant, as she'd never used that name with me before— "I could subdue you, drag you over to Cargill, and claim that that's where I found you. It's only twenty minutes away. It wouldn't be hard, and it would be the word of a rogue operator versus the word of the most famous superhero in America. No one would question me, and no one would ever know."

"Yeah, but you would know. Are you willing to risk your *honor and reputation* jailing the love of your goddamn life over a situation you're not even sure about?" We stared at each other for a solid minute. She was steeling herself to decide and I was steeling myself to fight through that decision if need be.

Suddenly, her shoulders slumped. It made me feel a lot safer but also a whole lot worse. I wanted to reach out to her, almost told myself to, but then she spoke again.

"As much as I hated what you did for a living, I never flat out told you to stop," she said with a little sigh. "At the threat of losing me, I could've...and you would've quit. But I let it ride because I trusted you. Even when I was mad at you, I always trusted you. You're not making that easy right now. If that's going to change, I going to need you to repay that trust."

"I can't...it's not that I don't trust you—" I wanted to tell her everything, but I took a moment and ran the scenario through my head, coming to the same conclusion Darryl always did: She's too high profile. She wouldn't just go back to working for that task force. She wouldn't pretend she didn't know. She'd feel honor-bound to help and that would draw attention to Mark. Marcie could protect herself, but Mark couldn't. The Imperative would go to ground, more hidden than they were now. The Sidana twins would be forced to camp out in that rec center until we could clear their names as persons of interest, which we couldn't do without proof of the Imperative's existence. The truth would cause more trouble than the lie. I saw now exactly why Darryl had made the decision to leave us. I knew why it was wrong, but also how it had been right.

Marcella, on the other hand, looked at me with tears in her eyes. "Is that all you can say? Even now?"

The fabricator finished its work and went silent. I looked at it and decided on my own.

"There's this." I grabbed the glass and swallowed the new Supercells in a single gulp. Then I looked Marcella in the eyes and waited for her to realize what I had done. By ingesting a fresh set of unformatted nanites, I'd basically reset my body's abilities. The new ones would reformat and disable the old. Without a way to reconfigure them to superhuman settings, they would maintain their default function of mimicking normal human cells. I would just be a regular person again. If there was ever a time when I was at my weakest, it was right now. If she took me down, I'd never bounce back. The sad look on her face told me that she understood all of that.

"So, what now then, Sana? Where do we go from here?"

"Look, I think this thing I'm working on is building to a head. I feel like it's gonna end soon. Let me go and see it through. Then we can talk. I know that's a huge ask. But it'll all make sense, I promise."

There was so much pain in her eyes. It almost broke me. "This was your chance to talk," she said slowly, finally. "This was your chance to make me understand. Your last chance. It's like you said, Sa, I'm the only one who knows that you're the operator that everyone is looking for. If anyone else figures it out, I'll get ordered to bring you in. When this local investigation goes nationwide, I'll put myself to the task of bringing you in. In either case, there's only one way this ends. You know how good I am at my job."

"I'm so sorry, Marcella." I was.

"Fuck you, Sana. You can tell the twins that I said the same...assuming you haven't killed them, too." She turned and walked out, leaving me alone and confused.

That last thing she said. Of course to her there was a possibility that Kani and Kazi were off the grid because I had killed them. To her, operators were immoral at best, soulless at worst. From her perspective, maybe this was me finally reaching my last bit of humanity and hatching a revenge plot where Hale got in the way. I didn't know whether to be offended or sad. My brain decided on both.

I wiped all the data that I'd used over the last few hours, shut down the equipment, and got in my car. I kept the windows down and the radio off. I wanted to retreat into my own head, but I didn't trust that Double M wasn't following me, not completely.

Chirp

"Sa, it's Darryl. You okay? You're behind the estimation I had for you getting back. Hurry up! We've made some major progress on two fronts. Great news ahead."

"Good. I need to hear something positive."

"What's wrong? Was the lab trip unsuccessful?"

"I made what we needed. I'll tell you all about it when I get back. Gotta concentrate on the road." I closed the connection between us and fixed my eyes straight ahead.

Chapter Nineteen

"There's a really basic class disparity between being a superhero and being an operator. If you're a low-level hero from a small town, you still get equipment and training commensurate with your location. If your profile goes up and you land in a big city, your equipment and training go up too. But most operators are self-trained and provide their own equipment. If they're poor at the start, they are at an immediate disadvantage competing against those who start off with means. The right gear can be the difference between completing a D-List contract and failing one. Which, of course, can be the difference between jumping up to C-List contracts and washing out of the industry completely. That's why rising in the ranks is harder for a skilled operator than for an equally skilled hero."

— *Dr. Carly Steif in* For Hire *magazine* — *April 2007*

By the time I got back to Columbus, the rec center was just opening for business. I had a key now but was glad I didn't have to use it. I gave Ronnie a nod as I walked past the front desk. He returned it. Getting to the back room, I found only Kazi there. "Where's the rest of the team?" I asked him.

"My sister's out for a run. Darryl's asleep," Kazi replied. I didn't like the idea of Kani going outside to run given the situation. But when she did she always wore sunglasses and kept her hair in a ponytail that she tucked into a cap. It was about as safe as she could make herself while getting out into the elements.

I walked over, leaned over his chair, and peered at his monitor. Porn. Of course. "What's the news? Darryl said you had a win for me. I hope he didn't mean this."

Minimizing the video he had running, he laughed. "Nah. That was just my own personal win. What I've got for you is job related. You want the big news first or the small news?"

"Big news first. I could use a big win."

"Yeah...no. I'm gonna give you the smaller news first."

"Why'd you bother asking then?"

"You're a smart girl. How was I supposed to know you were gonna answer wrong?" I rolled my eyes at that but held out a hand indicating that he should continue. "Darryl and I have been running simulations based on all the Imperative influence we could reasonably deduce. We checked through a lot of hacked communication too. When we cross-referenced the influence versus the times when the affected politicians privately spoke against their own coerced decisions, it became clear that The Imperative didn't or couldn't maintain prolonged control over their thralls. Their manipulation lasted just long enough to apply the changes they desired. Most of the affected would lose political capital if they waffled publicly, so instead they'd accept the

183

changes retroactively or just pretended to have had a lapse in judgment."

"Okay, so what's that mean to us?"

"If they're fucking with a lot of politicians and doing it regularly, it means they're local to Washington D.C. They aren't just visiting. They all live there. And based on Hale having the trappings of a real job...even for fake companies...we gotta assume the rest of them have public faces as well. They aren't kicking down the door with any of these politicians. They're being welcomed in for a legit purpose. Just like with Hale scheduling a meeting with my sister."

"So, whoever Circe and Araña are, they're hanging around on Capitol Hill. Pushing the buttons on-site. And even when they aren't in direct control, the folks they alter can't go back on their own words at the risk of losing the public trust. Awesome! How do we weaponize this information?"

"And that's the bigger news! We already have." Kazi pulled up a new window on his monitor and I recognized the video I saw there. The night I killed Hale, Darryl spent time recording video of the rest of the Imperative at the lobby bar in the Four Seasons hotel. That ballsy fucker even caught footage of himself leaning next to them, at the bar, ordering a drink. "Knowing that these two are both local, we showed the video to Kani. She said Circe was vaguely familiar, but she couldn't quite place her. Not helpful. But while our boy was waiting for the bartender to deliver his order, he heard bits and pieces of their conversation. Specifically, words like 'rigging,' 'topping,' and 'suspension.'" He clapped his hands and looked at me expectantly.

"Okay...should I recognize these words?"

"Kink!" he called out.

"Kink?" I repeated.

"Araña is kinky. I don't know who she is publicly, but privately she's a kinkster. The chains aren't just about her magic or whatever. She's into bondage and shit."

"And you know this how?"

"Because I'm into bondage and shit."

I shrugged. "Great. She's kinky. As none of us plan on dating her, how does this help us?"

Kazi rolled his eyes and went back to his computer. Opening a fresh tab, he logged into a website called KinkSpace. Its tagline read "A social media network for fetishists." A quick search later and we were staring at Araña's account. Aside from being part of a shadow government that selfishly and callously destroys lives, she was also an everyday girl with a social life. The profile gave us an unimpeded view of her fetish photos, her personal writings, and of course her RSVPs to certain D.C. area events. Bingo!

Just then, Kani walked in holding a bottle of water and mopping sweat off her forehead with a towel. "How was the trip? Did you see your mom?"

I paused, then decided *Why not*? "I saw Marcella." I said. "She cornered me in the lab."

185

"You two throw down?" Kazi said, turning his chair to look at me. Knowing him, he could be asking about us either fighting or fucking. I didn't want to know which, so I just shook my head. Kani snapped her towel at him.

"What my brother meant to ask was, 'How is she and did you two talk at all?'"

"From the outside, it was us as usual. She talked. I mumbled. But it's changed." I pulled out a chair and sat next to Kazi. Kani took it as her cue to sit as well. "She doesn't trust me anymore. She doesn't believe in me. She thinks I killed you both."

"What the fuck?" Kazi exclaimed, sitting up straight. "She really thinks you'd kill us? You were mad at us, yeah. But that's a bit much, even for you."

I shook my head. "Life as an operator isn't what you think it is. Sure, there's action and excitement and all that. There's also lying to my superhero girlfriend about the job from the night before. Or shutting my laptop when she walks in the room. Or showering the blood off my body right before she comes home to give me a big hug." I was met with blank expressions at that. "What I'm saying is there's been a lot of deceit over the years and she's smart enough to know when I'm not being straight with her. As far as she's concerned, she really doesn't know me at all."

"I guess that makes sense as to how she could believe you would...kill us." Kani needed to believe the best in all the people in her life, so her words hit me hard, even though all she was doing was agreeing with me. I guess I'd hoped they'd argue it. "What I don't get is why she didn't try to take you in. It doesn't sound like she even tried. Do you think she's okay with that? Us dying?"

"Well, you saw how mad I was with all of you. Maybe she's still holding on to that." I said.

"Yeah, but she's not like you. She's..." Kazi cut himself off. I scowled at him.

"What? She's what, Kazi? Finish the sentence."

"She's better at processing her pain in an emotionally healthy way," Kani said. She never stopped trying to save her brother. But I never stopped staring at him. He was gonna finish that sentence.

"I was gonna say, 'She's not a complete asshole.'" Kazi raised his hands in appeal for more time to finish his statement. I'd grant it, if only to watch him bury himself further. "Look, every group of friends has an asshole and you're ours." This was getting embarrassing. There was no save that Kani could've offered for that one. She and I both leaned away from him. My eyebrow raised. He shrugged. "Groups can have two assholes. I get that I'm the loud, brash one. But being distant and broody and dismissive to people that love you is some asshole shit too."

I was losing my patience with this. "Where are you going with this, Kazi? This isn't making me feel any better."

"You're an asshole but we love you anyway. Because even when you're distant and broody, you're also smart, occasionally funny, and fiercely loyal. You provide value to us that overshoots how unpleasant you can be sometimes. You stopped providing that value to Marcella, but that's temporary. This is a job and when it's over you'll have made the world a better place in a way that Double M's fists couldn't. That's the kind of value that makes up for eight years' worth of half-truths and lies of omission. You're gonna get her back, dude. And we're going to help you."

I sat with that for a moment. I took a deep breath and asked the real question. "Do I even deserve her back?"

"You do," Kazi said, and Kani nodded eagerly. "And whatever happens after this is over, we'll help you with that too."

Chapter Twenty

"A lot of operators get by because they have a support staff. I'm talking about the higher-level contractors. A- and B-List types that work regularly. They make enough money that they can hire normals with specialized skillsets. The kind of support that superheroes get as standard, some operators go out of their way to pay for. Personal assistants. Logistics folks. Strategists. People who can help operators but not be operators. It plays into some of the class disparities that exist. Even if it's just friends or family that get put on the team to get them out of a bad situation. Having people behind you can make all the difference."

— Dr. Carly Steif *in* For Hire *magazine* — *April 2007*

I couldn't tell if I was hungry or nervous. Maybe both. Hunger was an aftereffect of the new nanites. They always needed an increased amount of fuel during the proliferation stage when they first populated the body. That whole process usually only took four or five days and it had already been a week since I ingested the new batch. Either way, they were all set and configured properly. Even with the new neural link, I still wasn't completely used to how different my body felt. If it was nerves though? That would be a matter of my upcoming confrontation with an enemy I can't stand and trade blows with.

189

Also, being in a sex club.

Araña's calendar had her attending this event, which meant this is where I needed to be. No armor. Very lightly armed. My hair in a dark purple wig...like Marcella's. My skin slightly darkened with the help of makeup and a Supercell-induced pigment change, digital melanin being one of the special features of the new nanites. But unlike the rest of the team, who talked about schedules and locations and logistics, I spent more time studying her: her image, her words.

Araña wrote extensively about her desire to control and care in equal measure. She believed her own hands were the safest place for anything to be held...if she was never made to let go. Aside from all her other obligations, she worked full-time as a pro domme. Though she never revealed identifying characteristics, she often hinted at having a very high-profile clientele. The photos in her KinkSpace profile consisted of professional shots of bondage and domination scenes. The partners were always in masks or their images otherwise obscured. My guess was that they were made up of Washington's political elite. That would tie her together with some of the people we knew The Imperative had brainwashed. The same way Hale could set a specialized meeting, so could Araña. But nothing she wrote about any of her clients indicated what was really happening. Her writings were all thoughtful and passionate missives about people she viewed herself as safekeeping. That's why I was nervous about what came next.

As was my professional routine, I arrived far earlier than my mark, intending to get familiar with the environment. Before settling at the first-floor bar, I took two full laps of the entire location, making mental notes of all of the points of entry and egress. The club itself was a lovely venue with a classy interior that defied the shoddy brick face exterior. It was a two-story warehouse in Mt. Rainier, Maryland, just outside of the District. A place to get loud in a relatively quiet area. The building consisted of converted office space repurposed as a pleasure palace complete with an elaborate lighting rig that served to both hide and highlight. The floor plan was open and spacious with a large downstairs public area for voyeurs, exhibitionists, and sexually-disengaged socialization.

A DJ stood in the far corner. He was more of someone minding an online radio station playlist rather than reading the room and crafting a specific mood. In this place, the ambiance wasn't being generated by the music. Along the walls of both floors, the venue had several private rooms blocked off by moveable freestanding curtains. Each was stocked with a bowl full of condoms and packets of lube. A couple of the rooms even held a variety of well-maintained toys. The upstairs mirror of the public area was a dungeon full of racks, crosses, and leather strappy things. Kazi would probably love this place. I was just trying hard not to look out of place.

When Araña walked in, the mood changed, heightened. There was an air of formless anticipation that became a definite excited buzz upon her arrival. I wasn't the only one waiting for her. She was on a first-name basis with everyone who worked at the club. Surprising, seeing as how her KinkSpace profile indicated that she was an attendee at quite a few local play areas.

Everyone was glad to see her. She couldn't walk two feet without hugging or kissing or fondling someone who was clearly appreciative of the attention. She was mesmerizing. Her chains, I now realized, were so long that they didn't hinder her movement at all. She wore them under her clothes, revealing only the shackles at her wrists and ankles. Despite their obvious weight, she moved like water through the busy crowd. I imagined her magic allowed her a strength that defied her size. Another reason not to engage directly.

At one point, while crossing through the public area, she paused to take a glance at the scene of writhing bodies laid out around her. I studied her as she checked the clock on her phone's display. Deciding that she had enough time, she knelt and whispered something to two men who were playing together among a pile of other people. After both men nodded, Araña set down her bag, removed the loose dress she arrived in, and calmly inserted herself in between their naked bodies.

For all of maybe fifteen minutes, the three became a wild tangle of arms and legs and chains. Araña knew just how to wrap her links around the parts of her partners she wanted restrained. The men knew how to manipulate her bonds to position her to their mutual enjoyment. Their synchronicity was impressive. Each partner taking turns at using the other two, seamlessly transitioning from dominant to submissive and back. Satisfied by her short fuck-break, she kissed both men and replaced her dress before picking up her bag and heading to the stairs. The men resumed their pre-Araña activities. She was obviously very familiar with those two, but I got the impression that she could've picked any engaged couple at random and found herself welcomed. She owned this place.

I've observed dozens of targets, maybe even hundreds by now. None of them were ever this intriguing. It wasn't the scene, it wasn't the club, it was her. I couldn't keep my eyes off her and I wasn't the only one. The crowd pulsed around her whether they knew it or not. Once she got to the stairwell, I left my seat and moved in her direction. Following her up the stairs, I found myself as part of a building throng. Once I reached the dungeon, I understood why. Araña was once again removing the dress and pulling ropes, carabiners, and several impact toys out of her bag. Everyone wanted to watch the show, including me.

Like the images on her KinkSpace profile indicated, everything about her was professional. She, herself, was stunning. The tattoos on her body were an ordered composition of occult imagery. Not even one looked out of place and all were focused around a large spider inked between her shoulder blades. It was as if she had planned out the entire tapestry before the first needle ever touched her skin.

Her equipment was expensive, top quality, and well taken care of. She laid it all out like a mother laying her child softly in a crib. Everything was carefully placed in an order that allowed for ease of use. With Kazi's eager assistance, I'd researched the kind of gear that appeared on her social media feed, so I knew she didn't skimp. But I guess with the kind of money The Imperative hoarded, she didn't really have to.

As indicated in her writings, Araña was just as careful with her partners as she was with her equipment. Despite inflicting tight binds and harsh physical punishments on those she played with, she consistently checked in on their wellbeing. She easily navigated consent conversations and complex negotiations. She respectfully observed safewords and accurately read nonverbal cues. She knew how to use everything: The toys. The environment. The reaction of the onlookers. In this space, *she* was The Amazing Magisteria. All charisma and well-honed showmanship. Then she spotted me.

She didn't seem to recognize me from the hotel, thankfully, but she took an interest. As the night rolled on, I realized that she was only playing with people who arrived with other partners...and I didn't have one.

The crowd slowly thinned, leaving just a handful of onlookers. That's when she invited me to be her last partner of the evening. Apparently, her preference for topping partnered people was due to her desire to avoid breaking to provide aftercare until the end of the night. Instead, after each session, she released her participants into the care of a spectator they arrived with. She specifically reserved her own aftercare skills for her last.

I declined as politely as I was propositioned, and she thanked me for taking care of myself. I wanted to play with her. I wanted to put myself at her mercy. I wanted to receive her care. And she wanted all those same things with me. If you had asked me to list the feelings I expected to experience tonight, flattered wouldn't have made the top of the list. But there we were. She wasn't a monster, like Voss described. Or maybe she was, and I just see couldn't it. Here, to me, she was a charming, engaging woman. She was an artist...who also did monstrous things that hurt countless people. Consensually here and oppressively everywhere else.

That's why I stopped asking questions as an operator. I didn't want all this information. I didn't need to see the humanity in her. I could never separate the graceful poet with a flogger from the demon who fire-blasted me and Kani out of a hotel window. I had to kill them both.

After I declined, Araña didn't pick up any other play partners. Instead, she just got dressed and packed her gear. I excused myself, went to the bathroom, and splashed water on my face. I wasn't supposed to take my eyes off my target, but nothing about this night felt like standard operating procedure.

By the time I got back, she was packed and saying her goodbyes. The delay allowed me to close the distance between us. I was just out of her line of sight, but close enough to hear her chains clink as she moved. Just as when she arrived, everyone was appreciative of her personal attention. I cautiously followed her downstairs and moved towards my original perch at the bar as if I meant to stay there. As she reached the door, she turned to take in the room one last time. We caught eyes. She gave me a wink, a smile, and a small wave before exiting.

195

I was out of my seat and to the door before it finished closing behind her.

I hate this.

The streets were mostly empty and quiet aside from the traffic of a nearby highway overpass.

Between her thoughtful words and her intoxicating presence, I'd come to like her.

I lowered the density on my Supercells to make my footsteps even quieter.

I wanted to talk to her, to know her, to befriend her.

She was focused on her cellphone as I reached into my purse.

In another world, Araña could've been the Voss to my Marcella.

In this world, her throat was opened to the night air before she even knew I was behind her.

I don't want to do this anymore.

Chapter Twenty-One

"The critics always bring up murder. It's all they ever talk about it. But it's maybe 3% of total clearances for extralegal operations. I've been an active operator for over twenty years. I've been featured on the power rankings at least a dozen times. I was even number one for a couple of months back in 2002. I haven't made a single kill yet. Not a one! The critics are hypocrites anyway. Half of the politicians you see trashing operators only got re-elected because they hired contractors like me to jam up their opposition."

— *Operator Andy* — For Hire *magazine* — *September 2016*

For the next two nights, Kani slept in my bed with me. I barely got out of it. She brought me food, too. Instead of showing up with early morning status reports, she'd just been curling up with me each night while saying absolutely nothing. I needed comfort and support, she provided it. It's what she was best at.

Even without a previously established sexual relationship, if I asked, she most likely would've provided that too. But no. Typically, my contractor job provided me with both the necessity to unwind and the boundless confidence needed to easily navigate one-night stands and random hookups. But this wasn't that. And I didn't have enough people in my life that I cared about that I would exploit one of them as a means to an end.

One way or another, though, I wanted to feel something. I needed to feel anything, any other way. I had killed before, of course, but this was the first time I had ever thought of myself as a killer. This hadn't been on a legitimate contract. This hadn't even been in the immediate defense of a friend. And though I could logically understand that this was completely in service to the greater good, that her death undoubtedly saved countless lives, I still couldn't shake that I felt like a murderer. I wanted to feel like a lover again, someone capable of giving love and someone worthy of receiving it. But I doubted that was possible while I still had more work to do.

I needed this whole thing to be over. I kept seeing Araña every time I closed my eyes and sometimes when I didn't. Her breathless final gasp. The dawning of comprehension in her eyes when she lightly touched her throat and that touch turned red. The sound of her chains as she convulsed and fell over. I couldn't stop torturing myself by watching the scene play back in my head over and over. As much as I appreciate Kani's reassurance, it's not her arms that I needed wrapped around me. It's not her shirt that should be soaked in my tears.

I needed Marcella.

But whose fault was it that we weren't together, that we couldn't get through this like we always did? Mine. Darryl was right, again. I opened those emails. I accepted those contracts. I chose this life when I should've chosen her. I should've chosen Marcella the same way she always chose me. She found a way to love me when I broke up our superheroic duo. She stood by me when I started a career she found deplorable. She made it work even when I became all but a recluse. She fought for me while I took her for granted.

The upcoming election was only a few days away. The polls were starting to take notice of the candidates in local races. Mark was estimated to receive eighty-two percent of the vote. It was virtually a lock that late in the race. Once he won and started making waves, it wouldn't take long to connect him to wanted persons Kani and Kazi Sidana. For Circe, it might not take much longer to find a high school yearbook and spot the recently deposed, top-tier operator a few rows beneath Mark and several rows ahead of the twins. By that point, I was meant to be in D.C. providing the same type of coverage to Mark that Kani had the night I took down Hale.

It would be good to see Mark again even if the circumstances were shit. I wouldn't be able to communicate with him directly. However, he'd been given the same info package that Kani had and Darryl was able to send a comm-link out to Hewlett to plug him into the chirp line. Back in the day, he and I had shared a stronger rapport than I held with the rest of team, save Marcella. So, it would be good to see Mark again.

Darryl figured that we could just pull the same play that we pulled with Hale, except using our newly elected politician as the bait. I wasn't sure that would work, but I wasn't in a mood to argue or to discuss tactics at all really. Even when I was fit to be around people, all I did was hang in the background and take in news reports with the team. My friends were so used to my quiet lurking that they could pretend that things were back to normal for me. I was thankful for that. The only thing that could make me feel worse was being expected to talk about any of it.

The twenty-four-hour news cycle provided all our recent intake. We were essentially playing the waiting game, alternating between local voting information and updates on the now-nationwide hunt for wanted operators. The latter was chilling. Double M was amazingly efficient in her pursuit. She wasn't alone, but she might as well have been. The other heroes in the task force were just background players as she stalked state-to-state, cleansing the country of operators.

People I knew, or at least names that I'd become familiar with, from *For Hire*'s power rankings, were now regularly scrolling across the ticker at the bottom of the screen. Their faces began appearing bloodied, their bodies broken, as Double M carried them over her shoulder to waiting vans full of government agents. Every day, I expected her to kick in the door and charge in here. Darryl assured me that we were safe, but how would we know if we weren't? We could always be just minutes from a spot on the next news report.

The next part of our plan—if you could even call it that—required all of us to steer completely clear of Double M. If this played out the way we wanted, it would be over before she even had a chance to get in the way. We'd simply wait until the news reports had her listed as anywhere away from Washington, then Mark would publicly take shots at every single institution we knew The Imperative had a hand in. Then Circe would have to shut him up or lose all the ground she had gained. We'd be ready for either contingency. The real question of our success or failure would be answered by my willingness to retake the field. As much as I didn't enjoy all this down time, I wasn't eager for it to end either. I worried that this final kill would give me the same waking nightmares the last had.

Surprising absolutely no one, our boy won his election and was heading to the nation's capital to start some shit. I was supposed to give him time to get settled into his new office. After that, I'd start tracking his movement. I'd figure out where he was safe and where he was alone. Then we'd tailor a trap we could control for anyone who might seek to take liberties with our young political idealist. Surprising absolutely everyone, that plan got smashed before it could even get started.

The morning after the election, Kani was shaking me out of my sleep holding her tablet. Seeing as how she usually just hung out at the edge of my bed, eating breakfast, and patiently waiting for me to wake up, this had to be serious circumstances. The queued-up screen on the pad was running a live stream of a press conference getting started. The title underneath the video read, "Huge breaks in the Hale case/Operator War."

Before the shock of the headline had completely set in, Double M walked out and took up a position next to the podium. Her face was stern and her armor looked scuffed, the product of several fights over the last few weeks. Fixing, cleaning, or flat-out upgrading her tech was something we both did for self-care. The fact that Marce was still walking around in gear that was visibly scarred was an indicator of how much of herself she'd thrown into this effort.

To jump from shocking to downright surreal, she was followed to the podium by Circe her-fucking-self who approached the microphone and began to address the assembled journalists. "Good morning. We've amassed a great deal of information in a very short time. I'll just try to give you the essentials because time is a factor." She was wearing a suit not unlike the one she wore at the Four Seasons several months ago. A caption appeared on-screen that read *Secret Service Head Maxine Powell*.

How the fuck did I miss that? I knew Maxine Powell was the task force leader, but I never had a reason to look her up. I didn't have to. I knew her history. We all did. But she never appeared on camera. Intentionally so, I now understood. The one to see had always been the attorney general. The one to fear had always been Double M. Knowing that the person we were after was also in charge of the Secret Service and the one shutting down operators would've fucking changed things.

It wasn't just that Circe was within arms' length of several prominent politicians that we've researched, including the President of the United States. It's not even that Maxine Powell once had a career as the popular superhero Max Damage. It's that she'd been a mentor to Double M for most of her career. Powell was one of her inspirations for becoming a hero in the first place. But she wasn't a variant, gifted with extraordinary strength and speed, like we all thought. She was a mage granting herself those abilities.

I'd listened to Marcie's end of several phone conversations with the woman on screen right now, her pal Maxie. And somehow, I didn't even know what she looked like until ten seconds ago. How self-absorbed had I been?

No. That wasn't right. I mean, I *had* been self-absorbed, but I did know what Max Damage had looked like. She wasn't my inspiration, but Marce showed me the sexy pinup photos and the classic Max Damage comic books. The disconnect was that she showed me those years ago when we were teenagers. Further still, those collectibles were essentially ancient artifacts from well before we were born. The Maxine Powell I was looking at wasn't the same bombshell I remembered in the vintage baseball skirt. Clearly, upon retirement, she had taken off her long wig, put on a suit, and swapped out her baseball bat for a law enforcement baton.

Circe shuffled a few papers that I suspected were only props and continued, "As most of you are already aware, I've been heading up the task force in charge of shutting down the practice of extralegal operations and those who engage in it. Well, due to some new intelligence uncovered during Double M's investigation, we've been able to identify the murderer of John Hale as the operator known as JC or Jace Clementine. We've been able to discern that this operator's real name is Sana Rose Parker, originally of Rhodes and now of Cargill, New Jersey." Fuuuuuuuuuuck! Kani was stunned, too. She expected, from the headline, that the press conference would address her missing status. She didn't know the head of the Secret Service was about to plaster my face all over national television and the internet. Apparently, Marcella was surprised as well. There was a brief flash of astonishment across her face at the reveal of this new information. But it was just a moment, and possibly only recognizable to those who knew her best. Circe continued.

"I mention Parker's hometown as that seems to be the motivating factor behind her going rogue. It is our belief that John Hale was killed as he attempted to protect a friend and colleague, medical consultant Kani Sidana. Sidana and her brother, missing game developer Kazi Sidana, both originate from Rhodes as well. Both were high school classmates of Parker and we believe both to have been murdered by Parker. A third classmate from within the same friend group, Darryl Hicks-Brand, is being sought as a person of interest in this case. We believe he may also be in danger. If you have any idea of his whereabouts, please call your local authorities. It is literally a matter of life and death.

"Last but not least, my office has also received a credible tip suggesting that Parker is currently targeting newly-elected Representative Mark Jeffers, yet another high school friend." I sat back against the wall, stunned. By labelling me a rogue operator with three rogue bodies on me, she just made me Public Enemy Number One. My parents were probably watching this. Some asshole reporter was gonna harass my mother tonight, asking her how she could've raised a monster.

Max Damage—Maxine Powell—decided to make it even more of a challenge. "We've got the representative in a secure location for now, but Parker was once the best operator in the industry, leading the rankings for months. As much protection as we're giving Representative Jeffers, in the form of myself and Double M, it's possible that it won't be enough."

Just then, Kazi walked in holding his own tablet. "Are you watching this shit?" Kani raised her pad slightly. "This is so fucking fake! Who does this? She's airing out every fucking detail to the press! Why?"

"It's a trap." I said, my voice flat. "It's a trap for me. Circe knows that we're working against her now. Making me look like an unhinged operator with a high school grudge is a perfect cover for her when she kills Mark."

Darryl was right behind Kazi. "Wait! Why would she kill him?"

"Ummm...remember that time when we had to wrest the government from the hands of an opposing force? Well, it's kind of like that. But in reverse." Kazi was being sarcastic as usual, but he wasn't wrong.

I shrugged. "If she kills Mark, our plans are over. Darryl can only do so much from this building and the twins are both out of the game. If they come out of hiding, they become accomplices in my rogue activities. There's just no real way of proving that a former hero and current Secret Service head is also a mage who's been controlling the

205

government for decades. The only course of action we have left is to save Mark, somehow clear all of our names by exposing the entire conspiracy and stay out of Marcella's way in the process. No big deal. I'll get dressed. Tell Ronnie to warm up the car." Outside of holding onto anger, I've never been big on shows of emotion. I wasn't about to start. Not in front of them. I was spent. Tired. Broken. But they needed me to be a rock, so that's who I'd pretend to be for the moment—at least until I got to the shower where I could sob privately.

"They're playing it exactly like we played Hale. Do you think she's controlling Marcella?" Kani asked.

"She doesn't need to control her," I said. "She had to brainwash the president and the attorney general. If Darryl and Kazi are right and Circe can only enthrall one person at a time, all she needs is one or the other. But realistically, if it's Max Damage talking about civic duty, Marcella will do whatever she's asked."

"Fucking heroic bitch!" Kazi burst out. I cut my eyes and scowled at him. "Sorry, Sa. I meant it in the way I call you a bitch. The friendly way. I don't think she's a bitch, for real."

Best to ignore him, for all our sakes.

"Okay. So, if this obvious trap is obviously a trap, what can we do? What's our next move?" Kani asked, partially for information and partially to move attention away from her brother.

"The only thing we can do, Kan. I'm going to walk into their trap, save our friend, and walk out."

Chapter Twenty-Two

"There was this huge body positivity movement that stemmed, I think, from Max Damage's career. She had been doing hero work for at least a decade before she put on the red wig and the uniform she was known for. It was a tribute to some family member that played in the All-American Girls Pro Baseball League. But once she put it on and started doing pin-up style photo shoots, the appeal was undeniable. She was one of the first superhero sex symbols. Being a larger woman did nothing to diminish that. Then in 1992, they made that movie about the Girls' Baseball League. The star was a redhead and a couple of the main characters were fat women that weren't desexualized. I don't think it was a coincidence."

— Dr. Carly Steif in For Hire *magazine — November 2005*

None of us were happy.

Here's what we meant to happen: I was going to take a long shower where I would first cry, then steel myself for the upcoming fight, then eventually wash up. I would then carefully select my gear, then get packed and ready to go. Kani and Kazi, who were already showered and dressed, would save the last bits of relevant data to their mobile devices. Then, being good friends, they'd help me pack up my gear as we all prepared to leave. Darryl would shut down the remaining workstations in his command center, then give Ronnie a few last-minute instructions about the running of the rec center in his absence. Then the four of us would walk out to a van Darryl had stashed on the far end of the parking lot for just this occasion. Finally, we'd drive together from Columbus back to Washington D.C. for what we assumed would be the endgame.

What actually happened was Kazi came screaming into the bathroom. "We gotta go! We gotta go right now!" I had only gotten out my first good sob when his hand reached in and shut off the faucet. As the hand pulled back out, it grabbed then opened the shower curtain. With his other hand, Kazi shoved a towel at my naked body. "We. Gotta. Go. Now!"

Then he ran out. I followed, doing my best to get dry. In the sleeping area, Kani was on her knees hurriedly stuffing my gear into a duffel bag. She looked at her brother and pointed at two other bags. "These two are ready. Grab them and go downstairs. Help Darryl. I'm right behind you." She looked to me then indicated the bag she was holding. "Your armor is packed in here. Gloves too. If there's anything else you need, grab it fast. You got it from here?" I nodded, and she ran off to join her brother on the elevator before it descended.

I tossed the towel and snatched the first bit of clothing I could find. Kazi was always dramatic but Kani's frantic behavior made me take the rush seriously. I made sure to grab my boots, tablet, and phone. Everything else I had to leave to chance. The elevator back down to the command center felt frustratingly slow. I knew intellectually it was fast and only had one floor to go, but in this high-anxiety situation I might as well be waiting for it to be built.

When I got to the center, the twins were frantically pulling portable drives out of terminals and wedging them into overstuffed pockets. Darryl was hopping out of his chair to talk to Ronnie. "We're going out the back way. I started the Ninja Vanish protocol. Once we leave, this whole room will be locked down behind false walls, each embedded with a steel cage. No one should be able to see it or find it. Even if they do, it'll still take some effort to brute force their way in."

"Understood, Mr. Frost. What do you need me to do?" Ronnie stood up straight, his face so serious I almost wanted to tease him. Not the time.

"The protocol takes a while, maybe two or three hours to backup and wipe the lot. If they find this room, stall them. Stall them at least that long if you can manage it without getting yourself nicked. Most importantly, don't let anyone shut down the center. You know what this place means to the community. Protect it!"

"Absolutely!" He hugged Darryl and headed out to the front desk.

Darryl then turned to the rest of us. "It's about that time. Let's go!" He punched the last few commands into his terminal and hit Enter. All the room's lights turned red and began flashing. I could hear the panic doors start to slide into place as we left. Overburdened with unwieldy luggage, we took off through the back door and hustled across an empty basketball court to get to the exit. By the time we got to the parking lot, I could hear the sirens in the distance. My enhanced physiology told me that the police were probably still quite far, and we could all make it to Darryl's van with time to spare. My cautious nature told me not to take that time for granted.

From the outside, the van was just a van. A late model dark blue passenger van with wide windows, nothing out of the ordinary. Once the doors were opened, it was revealed to have three rows of seating, each outfitted with several jacks, plugs, and compartments. I also spotted logos for kinetic energy generators and data connection points. It quickly went from a standard transport to a mobile command center. Literally a command center for a series of mobile devices. Smart play, Darryl.

Once we had all the bags in, Darryl herded us into our seats like an impatient father. We all hustled to get in and get comfortable. The twins got in the second row together. I took shotgun. The rest of us got our respective computers arranged while Darryl started the van. He hit a button, turned a dial a few notches, then pulled out of the lot.

Feeling a bit more secure, I looked around from the front passenger seat and asked, "Okay, so, what the hell just happened. I mean, I got the general idea. But seriously what the hell happened in there?"

"It was the members of the club. They thought they were being helpful," Darryl said. I turned to look at him as he continued. "The rec center staff all know to stay quiet about me and anything they see me doing that isn't specifically linked to the center. I even incentivize it in their paychecks. The club's membership isn't sworn to that kind of secrecy.

"When our faces got put on the news, Ronnie and the crew started getting phone calls. People asking about my wellbeing. Even one from one of the ballplayers who saw us just after you roughed me up that first night. They wanted to make sure I was safe. The staff played it off, smartly enough, but at least a couple of the calls had to go to the coppers. And here we are."

"I'm just glad we got out before—oh my God!" Kani yelled, and I turned from looking at her to following her line of sight. She was looking at a parade of Columbus's finest. Several standard issue white police cruisers were accompanied by three SUVs and an armored SWAT van, each wrapped with a blue and red stripe across their sides.

"Steady, all. We're good. I'm just gonna pull off to the side and let them pass. Just relax. No heroics, Sana." He chuckled at his own joke and drove over to the left to park. It was the wrong side of the street, but the police had the rest of the road flooded. It was easier to just hop the lane to get out of their way.

The next few seconds were about as scared as I'd ever felt. If they recognized us in the van, this would be all over. We couldn't fight or escape all these cops at once. But if we hid our faces, it would be a dead giveaway. So we tried to keep from looking conspicuous while simultaneously trying not to be seen. That was until I peeked over at Darryl. He looked serene, smiling pleasantly with his hands at ten-and-

211

two on the steering wheel. I sat up straight and stared at the incredulousness of his behavior for a second before rolling my eyes and looking out the passenger side window. From the window of the third and final SUV, Double M looked directly back at me. Spotting me, she smiled her beautiful smile, then gave me a wink and a wave before returning her gaze to the road ahead of her. Out of habit, I raised my hand just before she looked away. But a second later, she was gone. All the cops were.

I was stunned. Shook! I turned around and the twins were similarly dumbfounded. Darryl, though, had burst out laughing as he took the van out of park and steered back over to the right side of the road.

"What the fuck just happened?" I asked. "Why aren't we getting yanked out of this van? Explain that shit!" In response, Darryl laughed even louder.

"Yeah dude. Why are you laughing? That wasn't funny. My heart is still in my throat," Kazi said. His sister was breathing hard, unable to speak.

"My friends, this van has been outfitted in the latest in optical illusive technology!" He waved his hands at the elaborate array of buttons and knobs that made up the van's center console.

"Your van has a cloaking device? And you didn't bother to tell any of us about it? You fucking dick!" Kani finally found her voice.

"Not a cloaking device. It's nanotech paneling on every painted surface combined with holographic imaging on the windows. Not too different from Sana's hard light shielding though not nearly as multipurpose. And of course I didn't tell you. Where's the fun in that?" He glanced up at the rear-view mirror. Despite how flippant he was being, I think he really wanted to see if she was okay.

"Okay...but Marcella saw me just now. She saw me! She fucking waved to me. What did she see?" I was still frazzled, but I was touching the windows and squinting at them trying to see if I could make out anything that might help me understand the holographic tech better.

"I switched to Responsible Mode before we left the rec center. So they all saw a silver van with a bespectacled middle age white man in the driver's seat, taking his car full of young children to soccer practice. Marcella didn't wave at you, Sa. She waved at a young fan who was shocked and surprised to see her. That's what they all saw. If their dashboard cameras caught us, they even picked up a false license plate number as well. We were never here, chaps." Satisfied with his own explanation, Darryl held up a hand and glanced around waiting for responses.

"That's...actually brilliant." I didn't want to give him credit, not after scaring me half to death with that stunt. But we were safe, and he was the reason why. Dick.

Kazi wiped the sweat off his forehead and gave a half-hearted laugh. "Brilliant and hilarious!"

Kani just scowled. "You're still a fucking dick, though."

"Thank you. Thank you. You're far too kind!" I could handle anything but the smug look on his face. I looked back out the window.

"How'd she get here so fast? The cops were local, but she was just in D.C."

"When you're the most famous hero in the country, you almost always have access. She never has a shortage of helicopter rides to private hangers with high speed, low occupancy airplanes." Something in my brain clicked and I realized what I'd missed. "Wait a minute! You said nanotech paneling. Since when do you know nanotechnology?"

Darryl feigned offense at the question. "I've got some background. I had some schematics. You may remember we did a little project together once..." He'd had nothing to do with programming or developing the nanites, so that wasn't going to fly.

"I remember that you got your schematics from me and your background is that you couldn't comprehend them. Judging by your current technical skill level, that hasn't changed much. So, who helped you with this? Not these two!" I pointed at the twins. "Are you letting people look at my stuff? Are you giving my tech away?" I couldn't tell how I felt about this. On one hand, I wanted to protect my intellectual property. Even if you had to be a very specific kind of genius to make sense of my work, the less people who had access to it, the better. On the other, this was really cool usage of the tech. Marce and I should've had chameleon-tech, custom-colored armor forever ago.

"Look, it's sort of a long story. I'll tell you later. I'm not trying to be evasive. Just now's not the time." He nervously looked at me then almost invisibly hinted towards the back seat. Almost invisibly.

From the back seat, Kazi started to guffaw. "Just tell her, dude. Tell her about your fake high school girlfriend." I recognized the reference from a movie Marce had me watch during happier times. I didn't recognize the context here though.

"Your one hundred percent real, not-at-all-made-up girlfriend that we've never seen because she lives two towns over? God, Darryl. No one cares who you're not fucking," Kani chided while reaching forward to clap Darryl on the shoulders.

"Wait is this finally happening? Oh shit, Darryl? Are you really dating someone? How come this is the first I'm hearing about this?" Whatever the story is with my misappropriated tech, I was genuinely happy that my friend had finally found...anyone.

"Enough! It's complicated and I promise I'll explain it all later. Can we just get through this first? We are literally running for our lives here. Let's just get where the fuck we're going. Quietly!" We shared a laugh together as we recognized my words thrown back at me. I blew a kiss to Kani in the back and she mimed catching it and holding it to her chest. As hard as it's been and even though it wasn't over yet, it was good being back around these goofballs. It felt like I'd finally recovered something I had lost.

Chapter Twenty-Three

"The name is actually bullshit. GVS. Genetic Variance Syndrome? The science doesn't support a single word of that. We don't know that it's genetic. No one's detected any variance. And syndrome? Fugheddaboudit! But some jerkwad reporter called it that back in the '60s and the name just stuck."

— *Vince Pirelli, writer for* For Hire *magazine* — *March 1991*

The laughter eventually died down. It had to. Our plan sucked. Darryl got worried about his rec center. The news reports didn't cover the raid and he dare not call Ronnie. Eventually, he switched seats with Kani. With her in the driver's seat, she and I could quietly discuss last-minute adjustments to my nanites and possible applications of their new functionality. The boys in the backseat could focus their time on finding answers.

In a three second message over the chirp line, Mark was able to pass us the address to the secure location where he was being held. It was likely the only information he'd be able to get out. The place was a million-dollar mini-mansion in the Colonial Village neighborhood of Washington, D.C. right on the edge of Rock Creek Park. Real estate websites and search engines held a wealth of floor plans, interior photos, and publicly available satellite imaging. I studied the available data. The place looked comfortable. Fairly secluded but not so isolated that passing cars or neighbors might be strange to see. I could live in a place like this. I could also spot several entry points to the property that might be obscured by the surrounding forest. I'd have to get on location before I chose a path or found a way into the house itself.

Kazi was able to pull off a miracle of hacking. The media didn't cover the law enforcement operation, but each member of the SWAT team had an earpiece and a body camera. Somebody was monitoring the play, possibly to give them direction in the moment. Kazi was able to tap the feed on one of the officers.

What we saw was typical of Double M. When she faced an enemy, she was the sledgehammer of justice. When she faced the public, she was something else. The police stormed out of their vehicles and rushed to the double doors that led to the center's foyer. Marcella called them to a halt, took the lead, and calmly walked in so as not to scare any of the club's members.

Instead of leading it like a raid and disrupting the location, she could be seen asking questions of the front desk staff, including Ronnie. We couldn't hear that conversation from our tapped officer's positioning. Eventually, M pointed at Ronnie and indicated that everyone else should leave, both the staff and the other officers. The cops all waited in the parking lot, just milling around for a few minutes, until Double M walked back out and called out that it was time to leave.

The rest of the trip went relatively smoothly, with no further run-ins with the law after the one we had in Columbus. Still, Darryl covered his face the one time we stopped for gas. It wasn't strictly necessary for the trip to Washington. We could've gotten there on the one full tank that we left Ohio with, but Darryl wanted to make sure we had fuel for our getaway plan. A getaway plan that, unsurprisingly, also sucked.

It sucked worse than the basic semblance of a plan that we had before Circe blew everything up. From the top: we needed to save Mark from the people holding him hostage under the guise of protecting him. That was my job. I needed to get in between him and them, giving him room to run out to where the rest of the team would be parked with the engine running. Foolish. Then their job would be to get Mark to safety and attempt to broadcast the truth, all while I tried to take down Circe. Simply moronic. And if Double M was also onsite, all of that would be impossible. She'd be fighting for Mark's life as hard as I was. She had loved him as much as I had.

If we'd had time to form a proper strategy, maybe we could've done better. As it was, the only thing we could do is show up and scrap. It was only a matter of time before Circe murdered Mark and blamed it on me. I assumed she hadn't already because she wanted to see if I would show up. Then, if she beat me, she could just hold up my body and use it as proof of my intentions. She'd be the hero that caught the rogue. If I didn't show up, I doubt she'd wait too long before killing him anyway, but then she'd always have to watch her back. Either way, it was a gamble. Especially now that we both knew each other's identities.

About an hour out from our destination, a light smattering of snow appeared on the ground around us. It got thicker and fluffier the farther we got into the DMV area. By the time we arrived in D.C., several inches coated every surface and it was still coming down. I was admiring the beauty of the winter and letting it calm me down when Kani pointed at our target. We were there.

We put the van in what Darryl referred to as Stealth Mode. A quick drive-by gave me the clearest confirmation that this was, indeed, a trap. There were no law enforcement agents near the house. No local police. No federal agents. Not even a security guard from a nearby shopping plaza. How could you claim to have a legitimate threat on a politician in the nation's capital but not have a single cop positioned around their home? Whatever was about to happen, Circe didn't want any witnesses. But there would be witnesses. Kani and I would make sure of that.

Even before our abrupt evacuation, the whole team decided to make the trip to offer logistical support. If this was to be an endgame, they wanted to play their part. Their presence gave me the best chance to pull off the hardest part. All I needed was for them to stay connected with me. Darryl's hacking of the property's wifi password would help. We'd only have one chance at this...and I'd most likely die in the attempt.

The team circled to the far end of the park and let me out. They'd go closer to the house to prep for Mark's escape. I couldn't help but be impressed by the van's stealth paneling. I had only just closed the door behind me and I immediately lost sight of the vehicle entirely. Darryl took care to keep the van centered in older tire tracks, so as to not create new ones. I saw a slight kick-up of snow, but I could only faintly hear it drive away as I started walking up to the secluded brick home.

My favorite set of light armor was specifically built for surreptitious approaches like this one. I wish it had some thermal lining though. Even with the undershirt I had on, I could feel every single snowflake that landed on me. It was so cold that I pulled on the hood that I almost never used. It was an added layer of protection from more than just the elements though. Hover-tech in my boots had me a few silent inches above the ground. My gear also packed enough light-manipulating hardware that I should be virtually invisible, at least if I didn't need that hardware to conjure a shield. That'd be useful when I got inside. I was closing in.

While I was almost positive that no one from the house could see me, I was dead certain that I couldn't see anyone inside the house. The windows were closed, and the shades were drawn. With my senses enhanced by the nanites, I could hear the magnetic resonance on the expensive door locks. Entry without disarming the locks would trigger an alarm.

Maybe upstairs I'd be able to find a better entry point. Finding a foothold on a porch-side banister, I leveraged my way up to a balcony next to what I assumed to be the master bedroom. Leaning towards a window, I heard something else. A conversation. Two familiar voices and one brand new one. It sounded...friendly.

I don't know what I was expecting. If everyone was in good spirits, I thought maybe I could get the drop on Circe and then reason with Marcella. Maybe I could—

The window exploded outward. A massive-gloved hand reached out and pulled me into the house. Before I could get my bearings, a second massive gloved hand collided with my head and I was flat to the ground.

"Stay down, girl." Of course it was her. I looked up to see Double M standing next to Circe. Mark was behind them sitting on a couch, surprised by the last few seconds of action. The television was flicking behind them. I couldn't hear it for the lingering ringing in my ears.

There was nothing I could really say that would stop what came next, but my plan was to get between them and him and that's what I was going to do.

Or maybe not. I was barely to my feet when Double M flew at me, Circe following close behind. She was shorter and stockier than Marcie, but she moved like a hummingbird. Quick, light on her feet, with a ballerina's grace. I was able to get off a single kick to Marcella's jaw before I felt a hand on my thigh then a baton in my gut. Then I heard a scream. Mark!

He was clutching a knife in his stomach. My knife. Taken from my sheath and thrown while I was reeling from the blow...and while Marcie was as well. Circe cried out, "M! The representative has been hit. She got him!" Either she was really good, or I just walked directly into that. Probably both. "You take care of her, M. I'll see to Jeffers."

I was flying out the window before I had even felt myself being picked up. The snow padded my landing, but the sound was far more muffled than my impact was cushioned.

The sound of crunching footsteps drew my attention back towards the house. I had to get up. I had to say something "Marcella...it's..." My head snapped to the side. I'd never been slapped before. Today seemed like a day for firsts.

"We've kind of taken this beyond words, don't you think?" Marcella said looking down at me. She was right. But we didn't have time and we didn't need words to settle this.

I dove at her...and missed. I recovered my balance quickly and threw a flurry of kicks and punches, none of which landed. The ones she didn't dodge, she passively blocked. I was overclocking my nanites and changing the settings every few seconds. Nothing helped. There wasn't a configuration that would give me the upper hand. I even swapped in her own default settings, the same ones I activated before jumping out the window with Kani. I used everything at my disposal. Three punch combos? Cartwheel kicks? Spinning back fist? All would've been instant knockouts against anyone else. I wanted to say that I was Eric Bana in *Troy* giving Brad Pitt the fight of his life in a losing effort. Nah. I was a toddler play fighting with her mom. If Marcella wanted, she could've grabbed my hands and slapped the shit out of me with them.

When I tried to grab her, she tripped me, spun me around and put me in a standing rear chokehold that was just about to end this fight. I was scrambling, kicking my feet and putting my hands anywhere I could reach, frantically looking to get a grip on...anything really. I was remembering everything I knew about her and came across two new realizations.

Firstly, she was better than me. I always had the impression that she was the strong one, I was the fast one, and that we were essentially evenly matched. But that just wasn't the case. Maybe we were balanced back when we first started. After all these years with me quietly taking people down by stealth and her diving face first into groups of criminals, she was just a more skilled and experienced fighter than I was. Stronger, faster, better.

The other realization was that I was slicker. Sneakier. Craftier. Regardless of what the ranking said, I was still the top op and punching people in the head wasn't how I got my spot. Exploiting my targets' weaknesses was.

Using the levitation tech in my boots, I launched my feet to make a single strong flip, straight up. It loosened the hold and altered Double M's equilibrium. When our faces were level, I bit her on the nose. It was the first thing that came to mind. It was the only bit of her I could reach. It was the only offensive move I had. It wasn't a hard bite, but enough to provoke a reaction. The reaction was shoving me to the ground with as much force as she could muster against the little bit of my body she could reach. The angle meant that her throw left her off-balance as well.

Perfect. I landed a good distance away and smiled to myself as I looked down to my right hand...which now held Double M's cellphone. She never bothered to change the hip compartment where she stored it. She probably kept the same passcode too. But that didn't matter because she never got around to removing my fingerprint authentication. I already had her phone unlocked with the Supercell app open before Marcella could even register the source of the digital illumination across my face.

"Give that back! I won't let you—" but it was too late. With increasingly numb fingertips, I drew the sliders straight to the bottom of the screen and shut her all the way down. Her last desperate lunge at me landed short, her body falling chest-first in the snow. Her now-average physique was encumbered by the weight of her equipment.

"Can I say 'I told you so' about the heavy armor?" I felt shitty saying it. It was ugly and seeing the moonlight reflecting in the gathering pools of her eyes made it even worse. I could be an ugly person sometimes. But that didn't mean I couldn't end this the right way. "I'm sorry, Marcella my love. But you've got this situation all the way wrong."

I could have thrown her phone off towards the tree line. In fact, I meant to. I could have run to the house and tried to end this while she was laid out right here. It would've been easier without her interference. But she deserved better than that. She deserved better from me. She always had. "Look, I want to tell you everything. I've always wanted to and I still do. I hope we have the chance after tonight. But right now, Mark needs me. He's gonna die if I don't get back in there. This is Phase Two. This whole thing has been Phase Two and I know this won't make sense to you, but Max Damage is the end boss.

"I may not be the hero, but I get it now. I get why you fight the good fight and I wish I had understood it earlier. All these years, I chose to prioritize my fears and my pain. Right now, this is me...choosing you. The way I should've from the very start." I took one last look at the phone before I dropped it right in front of her, right near her outstretched hands. Then I sprinted right back into the house with the tiny head start that I had allowed myself.

Chapter Twenty-Four

"We get a bad rap as operators. Yeah, you got superhero hot shots like Double M punching criminals in the face. But I probably take down just as many criminals as she does without a fan club or a line of action figures. Not that I want those things. But what she does with her fists in the armor, I do with my laptop in my underwear. Yeah some of us do some really heinous stuff on the clock. But a lot of us are prolific heroes who just don't want to be bothered with morning show interviews. We should get more respect."

— Operator Andy — For Hire *magazine — July 2017*

No need to be quiet. The prevailing silence told me all I needed to know about that. Harder to control the narrative if the alarm calls a bunch of cops to the scene of your well-planned cover up. The only people Circe was accounting for was the four of us: me, her, Mark, and Marcella. It's overconfidence like that that had been The Imperative's biggest flaw this whole time.

The only stealth I had left would've been ensured using the lev tech in my boots. I didn't bother turning them on. I only had one chance at this and it would be the Supercell's experimental new tech that would close this out.

I engaged the new features and hoped that they worked as planned. I wondered what the rest of the team was doing then. They still had their parts to play. There was no telling what I'd find when I got back to the room. Mark could be dead. Circe could be gone or preparing for a fight. Nothing I'd heard or seen, since getting thrown from the room, had given me any clue. Especially since most of my time back outside consisted of getting whomped by my girl. The sound of laughter hit my ears. If you had asked me to guess what I'd see when I got back to Mark, it wouldn't have been this.

Walking confidently into the master bedroom, I encountered a Circe who was...chilling. There was no other way to describe it. She was reclined comfortably on the room's sofa. Her left hand was wrapped around a beer and her right was sitting lazily on top of her baton. With her jacket removed and her sleeves rolled up, I could see the faint glow of the tattoos on her forearms. Her feet were propped up—oh God, on Mark, my knife at the center of a dark red halo on the front of his shirt. Circe was using him as an ottoman while she lounged around watching TV. On any other typical job, this moment of surprise would've been the moment for me to lean in and shoot her in the head. Of course, there was nothing typical about this job.

"What the fuck is this, Circe?" I kept my eyes trained on her. This was it. She turned her head but didn't bother to get up. As far as she was concerned, she'd already won.

"Oh, wow...it's you. I'm surprised and a little impressed. I really expected that goofy purple bitch to finish you off and get back here just

227

in time to have this asshole's death be the last thing I ever let her see."
She took a swig of her drink and smiled. "I'm also a little surprised that
you know that name. There's not a lot of people who do. I assume
you've been talking to—"

"IT DOESN'T MATTER WHO I'VE BEEN TALKING TO!" I took a
breath. "It's over. All of it. Your shadow government. The brainwashed
public figures. This bullshit war on operators. You're through." I didn't
know how long Mark would last, but I could hear him breathing. I
wanted to dive to his side and hold his wound close. I wanted to carry
him to a hospital. As the situation stands, I couldn't even spare him a
glance.

"Yeah, yeah, yeah. Check out how scared I look." She took a
glance at the TV and another swig of her beer before throwing the
bottle at me. I leaned out of the way, but my eyes never left my target.
"However you figured out that we've been influencing politicians? It
doesn't really matter. Hale and Araña were my friends, but they can be
replaced. I can find two others to take their spots in The Imperative in
no time. Running this country from behind the scenes is easier than it
looks. Brainwash any influential party leader, promote some radical
talking point, and this country will lean in to meet you halfway."

"Then why do you need to kill Jeffers, then? He's on the rise.
He'll be influential. You can use him. It's not like he can speak out
against you if he's under your control."

"Umm, that's your knife, with your prints, and my narrative, sweetheart. *You* killed Jeffers. Strange thing though...I can't control him. I tried. Double M either. Or you, right now, come to think of it. For some reason, my manipulation just doesn't hold on you three. But whatever, if you're here, Double M must be dead. So, *you* killed Jeffers, and *you* killed America's favorite guardian, and I...well, I killed you." Her smile became almost dreamy. "Not only am I a hero again. This time, I'm *the* hero: The hero of the Operator War. That'll get me in the room with all of this country's elite. Not just the politicians either. Even more access than I already had as a retired hero in the public sector. You've given The Imperative more publicity than I could've ever dreamed." I smiled at that. But I never let my gaze drop. She finally took her feet off Mark and leaned forward on the couch. "Y'know, I'd thank you...if I wasn't busy killing you."

She stood up with unbelievable speed and swung her baton at me. I was able to leap back easily but it was a feint. She meant to back me off, to give herself more room to work, and I played directly into that. A gun could clear that distance quickly, so I pulled out mine and unloaded on her.

I aimed each shot directly at her chest and watched them all harmlessly impact the wall several feet wide of their intended target. It was as if a wind blew each bullet off course. Whatever Circe had done to defend herself momentarily kept her from striking back. Powerful or no, she still had to build up energy she meant to expend. Not me though. I just had to act.

I grabbed a nearby coffee table with both hands, spun around, and used the momentum to launch it at her. Either the table would veer off course, like my bullets, and slow down her ability to respond or it would hit her with full force. I was already charging at her when a third option presented itself. Circe caught the table, just before it would've connected, directly in front of her face. The catch was slightly awkward due to her hold on the baton in her right hand, but it was still solid. The position of the table obscured her vision just long enough for me to close the gap between us and punch through the center. The momentum of the blow split the wood in half and my fist landed flush to Circe's throat.

The broken pieces of the table fell from her hands, but the baton remained. Though she reeled from the force of the impact and winced from the pain, this wasn't the one-hitter-quitter that I had hoped for. With my knuckles still mashed against her Adam's Apple, she lowered her head and, with strength that defied description, trapped my hand between her chin and clavicle. Taking a step back and leaning away, she pulled me in closer to a bear hug. The hold didn't last long as she spun with the motion she had generated and flung me clear across the room.

I landed violently against a heavy bookcase. My hard light shielding took the brunt of the initial collision but I definitely felt it. I also felt the weight of that bookcase as it toppled over and landed on me. A copy of Leo Tolstoy's *War and Peace* landed right in front of my face. I groaned, for multiple reasons.

I put my hands to the ground and did a pushup to rise to my feet. By the time I leveraged the bookcase off my back, I got a clear view of Circe. She looked a bit worse for wear—crouched over, struggling to breathe, but still standing. This was more of a fight than she was expecting. But the shimmer in the air surrounding her indicated that she got the results right before we even started.

Wearily, she raised her baton. In the distance between us, the furniture began to rise. Waving her arms in throwing motions, the couch came flying at me. I flipped out of the way, but wasn't able to dodge both broken halves of the table I had punched through. Next was the heavy bookcase again. This time it made to pin me against the far wall near the windows. I held up my arms, but my shields had already been weakened, first against M and then against Circe. With zero time to recharge, they couldn't hold up against all of this. Neither could my armor and neither could the nanites in my body. I didn't even see the next three things that hit me, but I assumed that fucking copy of *War & Peace* was one of them. I could feel everything going dark. So ended the short and illustrious career of Jace Clementine...

And then, out of the corner of my closing eye, I saw a flash of purple.

Chapter Twenty-Five

When asked about her newly claimed top spot in the operator power rankings, JC simply responded, "No comment."

— For Hire *magazine* — *March 2018*

"Nice shirt." I heard. It wasn't the only voice I could hear, but it was the closest and clearest and most familiar. Where was I? Every part of my body was sore, including the eyes that I was struggling to open.

"Huh?" I croaked out.

"I said, 'Nice shirt.'" I suddenly became aware of the fact that I was in my bra but not my shirt. I wasn't wearing my armor either. I couldn't see, but I could feel the cold against my bare skin. I could feel the carpet against my uncovered shoulder blades. I was alive.

When I finally cracked open my eyelids, I saw Marcella, goofy smile plastered on her face, crouched on her knees and holding my t-shirt in her hands. She turned it around to show it to me. As my eyes adjusted, I realized that it was actually *her* shirt. It was a retro Space Camp shirt that she loved. She wore it high and tight like a muscle shirt, but when I borrowed it, it just fit normally on my smaller frame.

"I mean, it's my nice shirt. It's just not what I call protection against magic. Same goes for this light blouse of yours." She laughed and picked up my armor. That's when I noticed her hands. She was wearing a portable Automatic Electronic Defibrillator embedded in a pair of gloves. It was the new tech that I built the night we argued in my mother's laboratory. But I took it with me and gave it to...?

I raised myself to an elbow and looked around the room. On a damaged but slightly usable couch, Darryl was typing furiously on a laptop. Kazi was tying Circe up in a series of unnecessarily elaborate knots. Kani was tending to Mark. She was speaking to him and her face was calm. He was going to be okay. I looked back up to Marcella. "You saved me?"

"Of course, I did, silly. I'm the hero."

Chapter Twenty-Six

"Attorney General Bobby Hollister has announced that he will be working with political advisor Darryl Hicks-Brand to form an accurate pattern of behavior to attribute to the criminal mastermind Maxine Powell, also known as Circe and Max Damage. A reliable map of the coercion and intimidation caused by the group calling themselves The Imperative has been hard to establish. In the aftermath of the assassination attempt on Representative Mark Jeffers, elected officials have been rushing to use the bizarre circumstances as a justification for their most unpopular decisions. As of right now, Powell's confession, which was broadcast live to the internet in real time, is the sole piece of evidence that is keeping her behind bars. Her lawyer is claiming it to be a fabrication and is looking to have it thrown out of what is sure to be the court case of the century."

The news reports had been non-stop about the event, which everyone was still calling The Operator War. Could you blame them? America just found out that its government had been compromised at its highest levels. I was kind of over it, though. If there wasn't a crowd of afternoon regulars stacked around the TV at Luke's Lockup, I'd just turn it off and forget the whole thing ever happened. Instead, I was hunched over a plate of cheese fries with the woman I love, lamenting my newfound notoriety.

"Okay. I'll start. How much did you rat me out?" I took a fry and stuffed it in my face with a smile.

Marcella sighed. "Just a little. You're gonna laugh but I gave up your code name. Your original code name. Your superhero name."

I didn't laugh. I groaned. "You're kidding! It was such a bad name. I meant to take that to my grave." I took a sip of my beer and lowered my voice a bit. "Why'd you tell them anything? Or, if you were gonna talk, why didn't you tell them more?"

She looked down and put her hands on the table. She twisted her fingers around themselves. All these years and I've never gotten used to seeing this giant of a woman look sheepish—on the rare occasions where it happened. "I was still torn, babe. Maxie was my friend and my mentor. And you're...you. I didn't want to out you completely and I couldn't pretend to not know you at all. So I gave up your original code name and just let it be assumed that we lost touch after our duo ended. When Maxie revealed your operator alias, your real name, and your hometown? I was shook. I had no idea she had all that information." Scanning my face and seeing that I wasn't mad, she quickly relaxed again. She picked up a fry and pointed the cheesy end at me. "And I thought your old name was cute. I gave you that name."

I smirked and watched her clear the fry in a single bite. "Fine. It's still humiliating though. Your turn." There were so many details that we'd missed by being so far apart. The news reports helped. Marcie had been watching them all then coming to me for the specifics. But it was time to have a clear-the-air session about a few of the finer points. And cheese fries.

Luke had always done a great job of warning other patrons away from bothering me in my corner booth. I was shocked that it was still holding up, given that Double M was with me. But that gave us the time to cover all the important stuff.

"Soooo, you were really that little girl?" She laughed. "The soccer player in the minivan that I waved to in Columbus? Kazi said that was you. Are you fucking kidding me?"

"It's true. Darryl's van has a cloaking device. He calls it something else, but it's totally a cloaking device. He didn't tell us either. I thought we were caught when you looked right at me. We all did. The twins almost pissed the backseat." It was fun to be able to laugh about times that were petrifying in the moment. The next fry I picked up was really two fries stuck together. I attempted to wiggle my choice free of its gooey brethren. "Okay, so my turn. How did you get that kid Ronnie to turn? You talked to him alone for like five minutes and it looked like he gave you answers."

After examining my futile efforts, Marcella just reached out and delicately peeled the second fry off the first. "Ronnie didn't turn," she said. "The kid was a rock. He just had a lousy poker face. I cleared the room to get rid of all the noise and I studied him. I questioned him and just watched his reactions. He didn't even answer half of what I asked. By the end of our 'conversation,'" she put up air quotes, "he 'told' me that you and Darryl left together, that you were both in danger, and you were heading back to Washington. I read the poor kid like a book. He was so ashamed of himself. Even I was a bit embarrassed for him. It's the whole reason I beat you back to D.C. If he had held a straight face better, I might've spent hours tearing that place apart looking for you. I hope Darryl isn't too hard on him." She picked up her mug and gulped down the contents in one extended swallow.

Pondering the turn of events, I realized that I'd been extremely lucky. "I should thank him, then. His bad acting may have saved my life."

She slammed the mug back down to the table and pointed at me. "Saved your life. But only after it secured you an ass-whupping that you rightly deserved."

I don't care how much I deserved that beating, there was no way I was letting that slide as-is. "An ass-whupping I deserved in a fight I ultimately won." We stared at each other as I slowly sipped my drink down to the bottom of the mug. There's that tense moment between friends where we could be joking or fighting. I took the initiative to dial it back to joking before Marce considered asking for a rematch. "Y'know speaking of Darryl. He's seeing someone."

Tense moment diffused. Her eyes went wide as she covered her mouth with her hands. "Get out! Who?"

"I have no idea. He says it's complicated and the twins were giving him shit about it. But I'm dying to get the details." We had gotten to the point of the cheese fries where there were no more dry ends to grab if we were going to continue eating with relatively clean fingers. It was either use a fork or get my hands dirty. I chose the former.

My girl, of course, chose the latter. "Darryl dating? It's a new day indeed! But it's my turn again. What's with you and Charlie?"

"I—I don't know." She frowned at that. I couldn't blame her. Not after everything I had kept from her. "I'm not trying to be evasive and some of it isn't my truth to tell. But what happened with Charlie and I was unexpected. It really did start as just a random hookup. Then it took a left turn into something a bit more complicated. They really came through for me when I needed a friend who understood magic. When I needed a friend, period. You know how long it's been since I let myself connect with anybody? But we haven't spoken since just after you saw me at that show. I'm sure we will though." I dug my fork into the remaining fries and pulled back a trio of soggy potatoes. I held the utensil straight up and considered the contents. "So, I really don't know what's with me and Charlie. I suspect our next threesome should be pretty epic though."

She was wearing her "I told you so" smile. I could tell she was glad I'd found another meaningful connection. Thankfully, she didn't rub my nose in it. "See? There's the kind of wholesome conversation I come to dive bars for."

"This is not a dive." I made a face at the disparagement of my favorite haunt. "But I guess when you're super famous, anything less than four stars is a dive."

"Careful! You're a little famous too now." She pointed a cheese-coated finger at me, then lifted her hands in a grand gesture. "The operator who broke the story of the century. Darryl tells me there's talk of retroactively listing your entire takedown of The Imperative as a single op. It would get you out of having to testify in court and it would likely restore your top spot in the rankings. There isn't a single operator that would challenge it either, seeing as how your work is securing the release of so many wrongfully imprisoned contractors."

I looked down. If I had to think about it, I guessed I was happy with the overall results. But Marce put her heart into a false crusade. That was a rough place to find yourself. "How's all of that sit with you?"

Her smile softened. "Surprisingly well. Regardless of how I feel about extralegal operations, it's the law of the land. The releases are just. What I'm not as okay with is the apology tour the attorney general wants to go on."

I lowered my fork. "Apology tour?"

"That's not what they're calling it. But that's what it feels like. He's going to travel the country and play contrite over the Operator War. I'm supposed to go with him and make nice with the folks I put away. I'm the only one being asked to. But I didn't do anything wrong. I was given a job that I believed in and I did that job extremely well."

I thought about remarking on how much that sounded like something I'd say. Making this about me probably wasn't the most supportive move. Plus, she was clearly hurt at being thrown under the bus and I'm sure she didn't have a lot of people to talk to about this. "Make nice? Like how?"

"I'm supposed to shake a lot of hands, welcome people back to society, use my celebrity to perform friendly gestures. Most of these operators are looking for autographs and signed selfies from me. A couple are even demanding that I take them out for dinner. All of this to avoid a bunch of costly lawsuits for shit that wasn't our fault." It sounded like tedious work. Even for someone so committed to having a personal touch. But I couldn't place her frustration beyond basic annoyance at the pointlessness of her next task.

"If the releases are just and you're doing stuff for your fans that you do all the time anyway, what's the problem then?"

"The problem is that I do that stuff because I love my job and I love my fans. Not because I'm expected to. Not because I'm ordered to. It's times like this that I envy the freedom operators have. I mean, we all got played here. We should be fixing the system. Not apologizing for being tricked into breaking it."

"I don't know that it really costs you much more to do both as opposed to doing one or the other. But I get your point. Whose turn is it?" There was nothing left to be gained by sticking to this point. Not for either of us.

"Yours." Her tense shoulders relaxed at the shift in dialogue.

"Okay. So what's now?"

Marcella raised an eyebrow. "That's a pretty broad question."

"Well, you're a pretty broad," I said in my smarmiest voice. I followed up with a wink and a pair of finger-guns.

"That was awful. Literally the worst. For that joke, you're gonna buy me another drink. To answer your question, though, what's next is I get outfitted with whatever upgrade you're running. During our fight I noticed you switching configurations on-the-fly without the mobile app. Not to mention recording and broadcasting Maxie's confession with your eyeballs. Whatever you've got? I want it."

"Of course. Kani and I can get you set up. But that's not what I meant. I'm talking about the work. I do something you hate. You do something that boxes me out of your life. If you asked me to stop, I would. I don't want to kill anymore but I still like the nature of what I do. Even though the circumstances get muddy at times, I love the independence of it. I'm also not willing to chance losing you again. Especially now that I'm reconnecting with everyone else. But I love my job and I love my girl. I want both but you're my priority."

Marcella looked down at her mug, her expression blank. "I'm your priority?"

"Yeah."

She turned the mug around in her hands. "You're going to prioritize me?"

"Yes." I said, growing impatient.

"Well, my empty mug doesn't believe you." She was stalling for time. I gave it to her. We eventually had to get here.

Without another word, I picked up her glass and mine. I slid out of the booth and walked over to the bar. From the far end, where he was talking to the other patrons, Luke gave me a glance over his shoulder. I gave him a head nod and raised two fingers. He returned the nod, finished his sentence, and moved to fill up two fresh mugs.

The TV was still showing my face on the news. My face and my footage. Darryl got it out to the media as soon as I broadcast it through my nanites. The new features surrounding my vision and my memory were great, but I doubted I'd use them a lot going forward. I spent too much time agonizing over Araña but with footage and recall? I didn't know if I'd ever get past it. Despite wanting to return to work, I wasn't eager to revisit that feeling.

My attention was jostled by a hand firmly clapped on my shoulder and left there. I was standing between two regulars; I recognized both but knew the names of neither. The man to my right was looking up at me. It was his left hand on me now. Before I could shrug it off and confront his rudeness, he slurred out the words, "God bless what you did out there. You're a real hero!"

But I wasn't a hero. Outside of my job as a not-hero, I was barely a fully functioning human most days. I lived my life being incompatible with fully functioning humans. This guy was making all these assumptions because of the media hoopla. Assumptions of knowledge. Assumptions of access. Assumptions of familiarity. This guy didn't know a single thing about me or what I've been through. And he really shouldn't have been touching me. I wanted to say all of that just as Luke popped up with my drinks. Instead, I just said "Thanks," then picked up the new mugs as soon as the bartender let go of them. That must be what Marcella dealt with all the time. Responding politely to people getting a little too comfortable with her. Except she thrives on that kind of well-meaning interaction. Like the one that appeared to

242

have sparked up in my absence. As I returned to our table, I saw someone sitting in my seat. Not a regular, this new person was maybe a shade older, wearing a lovely dress, and with hair grown out into locks. They were chatting excitedly with Marcella, who was calmly taking it all in. It reminded me of the two of us growing up in Rhodes. Marcie talking my ear off. Me just listening. A mostly eaten plate of cheese fries between us. This surprise addition to our booth had just slid a magazine across the table. Drawing near, I saw that it was a dogeared copy of *For Hire*. The same issue I was reading when Charlie first approached me in this same booth.

Marce turned her head to acknowledge me as I set the new drinks down. "I made a new friend while you were gone. Sana, this is Imani. They spotted my hair from the street as they were walking by and came in to meet me. Look at what they had stuffed in their backpack." Marcie held up the magazine to show me before pulling out a pen and signing the cover. "Aside from being thoughtful and observant and quite well-dressed, Imani here is a variant. They're trying to figure out what to do with their abilities. If anything at all. I said they could ask us a couple of questions. Is that cool?"

"Yeah, of course." I slid back into the booth opposite of my original seat. Marce scooted down to make room for me. It felt weird facing away from the door, but I was sure I could turn off the paranoia for an afternoon.

"Thank you, Double M! Thank you so much! Can I get that picture first and can I put it on my social media feeds? Otherwise my friends won't believe I really met you." Marcella nodded. Imani got up, pulled out a phone, and gauged the lighting to prepare for the impending selfie.

"Of course, post it wherever you want and be sure to tag my official fan club." Marce said. I moved to vacate the seat I just got settled into when she threw an arm around me and held me close, "But let's both get in on that picture."

"Are you a superhero, too?" Imani asked me as they angled the camera to fit us all on the screen.

Marcella held up the copy of *For Hire* in view for the photo then said, "She's no superhero, Imani. This is my girlfriend and she's the best operator there is!" Before I could react, she planted a huge kiss on my cheek and Imani snapped the picture.

About the Authors

Kevin Patterson, M.Ed has been practicing ethical nonmonogamy since August of 2002. In April of 2015, Kevin was inspired to start Poly Role Models, a popular interview series blog. The blog extended into speaking engagements about how race and polyamory intersect and the writing of the book, Love's Not Color Blind. Kevin took a month-long break from Love's Not Color Blind to write the first draft of another book. You're holding it.

Alana Phelan is a librarian, writer, editor, and community organizer. She lives in South Jersey with her family, two cats, and a surprisingly large Dorbz collection. You can find her online as The Polyamorous Librarian, where she writes a weekly advice column and offers workshops and relationship support. She wasn't supposed to be a co-writer on this book, only an editor, but here we are.

Where can you find us?

For Hire
Facebook.com/ForHireMag
Twitter: @ForHireMag

Kevin A. Patterson
Facebook.com/PolyRoleModels
PolyRoleModels.tumblr.com
Patreon.com/PolyRoleModels
Twitter/Instagram: @PolyRoleModels
YouTube: Poly Role Models
PolyRoleModels@gmail.com

Alana Phelan
PolyamorousLibrarian.wordpress.com
Facebook.com/PolyamorousLibrarian
Twitter: @HelloLibrarian
Patreon.com/PolyamorousLibrarian

Acknowledgements

We couldn't have made this launch run as smoothly and as successfully as it has without a ton of support from the people who backed us on IndieGoGo! Endless appreciation and we hope you loved the book!

Kat Stark

Briar Harrison

Dawn Patterson

Marla Stewart of Velvet Lips

Hannah Rainier

Lynne Hernandez

foXXXy contin

Shawn Poole

Manjari Olds

Ray Henry

John Morella

Jeremy Peirce

Sean Holmes

Jase Lindgren

Thomas Limoncelli

Vince Zamora

Tracy Omagbemi

Colby Agostinelli

Yoni Alkan

Intimacy ConAmore

Steven Feldman

Sara Reed

Eve Rickert

Mary Crauderueff

Devlin Mckee

Ashlei Perry

Team Garzhammer

Rebekah May

barbs

Semona Baston

Kevin Hogan

Lacey Stewart

Apurva Desai

Robin Renee

Rebecca Newman

Kaiya Pinto

Kenton Johnston

David LeBer

Derica Brown

Athena Affan

Ian Pinsker

Rachael Amen

Carly S.

Satchmotron

Jessica Pryde

Laura Warnecke

Elizabeth Pepe

Hermione Danger

Brandon L Oglesby

Jim Donsky

Michael Guichet

Katrina Fraley

Annie Ng

Letitia Dixon-Coombs

Terri Stevens

Ellesin

Rachael Brunner

Dr. Liz Powell

Amanda Hacking

Murphy

Morgan M.

Aubry Costas

Lauren Graf

Ashley Erb

Stephen Wright Jr

Keira Harbison

Dawn Leinberger

Imani Thomas

Shawna Jaquez

Also Available from Kevin A. Patterson

Love's Not Color Blind: Race and Representation
in Polyamorous and Other Alternative Communities
From Thorntree Press

"It's incredibly hard to talk about racism with people who are not receptive to education. Kevin does amazing work in this book both centering the voices of people of color and educating white folks on privilege. His words will positively influence polyamorous communities for years to come."
—Rebecca Hiles, *The Frisky Fairy*

"Kevin Patterson uses everything from pop culture to scientific studies to open your eyes to a different perspective. The lens shifts from an angle of separation of subculture to a focus of centering. As a sex-positive event planner, I need all the tools I can get in order to ensure our events are inclusive. As the author says, 'If you aren't being *actively inclusive, you are being passively exclusionary.*'"
—Kendra Holliday, writer and editor of *The Beautiful Kind* blog, co-founder of Sex Positive St. Louis

Sana and Marcella will return...

45126200R00150

Made in the USA
Columbia, SC
28 December 2018